A Whisker
in Time
by

Kathi Daley

I want to thank the very talented Jessica Fischer for the cover art.

I so appreciate Bruce Curran, who is always ready and willing to answer my cyber questions; Jayme Maness for helping out with the book clubs; and Peggy Hyndman for helping sleuth out those pesky typos.

Thank you to Nancy Farris, Darla Taylor, Taryn Lee, and Pam Curran for submitting recipes.

And, of course, thanks to the readers and bloggers in my life, who make doing what I do possible.

Thank you to Randy Ladenheim-Gil for the editing.

And finally, I want to thank my husband Ken for allowing me time to write by taking care of everything else.

Books by Kathi Daley
Come for the murder, stay for the romance

Zoe Donovan Cozy Mystery:
Halloween Hijinks
The Trouble With Turkeys
Christmas Crazy
Cupid's Curse
Big Bunny Bump-off
Beach Blanket Barbie
Maui Madness
Derby Divas
Haunted Hamlet
Turkeys, Tuxes, and Tabbies
Christmas Cozy
Alaskan Alliance
Matrimony Meltdown
Soul Surrender
Heavenly Honeymoon
Hopscotch Homicide
Ghostly Graveyard
Santa Sleuth
Shamrock Shenanigans
Kitten Kaboodle
Costume Catastrophe
Candy Cane Caper
Holiday Hangover
Easter Escapade
Camp Carter
Trick or Treason
Reindeer Roundup
Hippity Hoppity Homicide
Firework Fiasco

Henderson House
Holiday Hostage – *December 2017*

Zimmerman Academy The New Normal
Zimmerman Academy New Beginnings
Ashton Falls Cozy Cookbook

Tj Jensen Paradise Lake Mysteries by Henery Press:

Pumpkins in Paradise
Snowmen in Paradise
Bikinis in Paradise
Christmas in Paradise
Puppies in Paradise
Halloween in Paradise
Treasure in Paradise
Fireworks in Paradise
Beaches in Paradise
Thanksgiving in Paradise – *fall 2019*

Whales and Tails Cozy Mystery:

Romeow and Juliet
The Mad Catter
Grimm's Furry Tail
Much Ado About Felines
Legend of Tabby Hollow
Cat of Christmas Past
A Tale of Two Tabbies
The Great Catsby
Count Catula
The Cat of Christmas Present
A Winter's Tail
The Taming of the Tabby

Frankencat
The Cat of Christmas Future
Farewell to Felines
A Whisker in Time
The Catsgiving Feast

Writers' Retreat Southern Seashore Mystery:

First Case
Second Look
Third Strike
Fourth Victim
Fifth Night
Sixth Cabin
Seventh Chapter

Rescue Alaska Paranormal Mystery:

Finding Justice
Finding Answers
Finding Courage
Finding Christmas – *December 2018*

A Tess and Tilly Mystery:

The Christmas Letter
The Valentine Mystery
The Mother's Day Mishap
The Halloween House
The Thanksgiving Trip – *October 2018*

The Inn at Holiday Bay:

Boxes in the Basement – *November 2018*

Haunting by the Sea:
Homecoming by the Sea
Secrets by the Sea
Missing by the Sea
Christmas by the Sea – *December 2018*

Sand and Sea Hawaiian Mystery:
Murder at Dolphin Bay
Murder at Sunrise Beach
Murder at the Witching Hour
Murder at Christmas
Murder at Turtle Cove
Murder at Water's Edge
Murder at Midnight

Seacliff High Mystery:
The Secret
The Curse
The Relic
The Conspiracy
The Grudge
The Shadow
The Haunting

Road to Christmas Romance:
Road to Christmas Past

Chapter 1

Friday, October 26

The dark hardwood floors shone brightly as the first patrons entered the newly remodeled bar my brothers, Aiden and Danny Hart, had sunk all their money as well as all their time into. While O'Malley's had been the local watering hole for quite some time, after years under the same ownership it had begun to feel tired and somewhat dated. When the O'Malley family came to the decision to move to Boston, Aiden and Danny had decided to buy the bar, refurbish it, and make it their own.

And what a facelift they'd given the place! The scuffed and faded wood floors had been sanded and stained in a dark walnut to match the original bar, which now had to be considered an antique by anyone's standards. The old rickety tables and wobbly chairs had been replaced with new furnishings in a much lighter shade. The natural wood walls, which had previously been dark and dingy, also had been sanded and stained, this time with a rich pine finish. The most dramatic change, however, was to the old back wall, which had featured a black metal door leading out to the back deck. My sister Siobhan had suggested that the brothers replace the metal door with large glass sliders, which would bring in more natural light and a new element if placed on either side of a floor-to-ceiling brick fireplace. The doors, along with the additional accent windows that had been placed along the entire wall, brought in the feel of the outdoors, while a low-maintenance gas fireplace provided a warm, cozy feel during the colder winter months.

The place, in a word, was fabulous.

"It looks like the whole town came out for the grand opening," my best friend, Tara O'Brian, said to me. Tara and I, along with my sisters, Siobhan Finnegan and Cassidy Hart, my fiancé, Cody West, and my brother-in-law, Ryan Finnegan, had volunteered to help out during this important event.

"I knew people were excited about seeing what the guys had been up to, but even I have to admit the turnout is better than I could have hoped."

"I guess the real test will be whether the guys can retain the steady local business O'Malley always was able to depend on," Tara commented as we loaded pints of beer on a tray for delivery to the tables to which we'd been assigned.

"Danny and Aiden have been customers at the bar for years. They know all the regulars. I think they're going to do fine."

I looked around the crowded room. As I'd predicted, many of the bar's regular customers had shown up and were holding court at their usual tables. Chappy Longwood was an old and weathered fishing captain who'd worked the waters surrounding Madrona Island since before my brothers were born. He was retired from commercial fishing now, but it wasn't unheard of to find him out on the water, reeling in his own dinner for the evening. Chappy was in many ways considered to be a fixture at O'Malley's. He liked to sit at the bar and chat with whoever was tending bar on any particular day.

Edwin Brown, a retired history teacher who'd worked at the high school when I was a teenager but had since retired, liked to set up camp in the corner by the window. He was currently running for island council and used the bar as a place to meet with voters and campaign for the seat. He usually showed up early with a book. He liked to read the classics while he waited for his fellow islanders to arrive, but once he had an audience, he worked the room so effectively, you'd assume he'd been in politics his entire life.

And then there was Pops McNab. Pops had lived on the island since before my father was born. I had no idea how old he was, but I was certain he must have passed his eightieth birthday years ago. Pops liked to talk about the Madrona Island of his past, and most of the regulars who spent time at the bar enjoyed listening to his often-far-fetched stories.

Yes, I decided as Tara and I picked up our trays and walked through the crowded room, the regulars had shown up in an offer of support. Both Aiden and Danny were behind the bar, filling orders and chatting with everyone who came in. Cody and Siobhan were helping Cassie in the kitchen, while Finn stood near the front door, ready to take on the role of bouncer if necessary. Tonight truly was a family affair, but after this, Danny and Aiden would have to make do with the staff they'd hired, including two new waitresses, Stacy Barnwell and Libby Baldwin. They were both running a mile a minute, so I'd pitched in to help deliver drinks. I'd just emptied my tray when someone bumped into me from behind, almost knocking me onto my backside. I turned around only to come face-to-face with the last person I wanted to see.

"Monica," I said with the sweetest smile I could muster. Monica Caldron had gone to school with Cody and Danny. She'd been, and still was, a beautiful woman who'd dated both my brother and my fiancé before leaving the island a decade ago. When I heard she was back, I was cautious. When she told me right to my face that she planned to seduce Cody away from me and would offer proof that she had, I was furious.

"Well, if it isn't the soon-to-be-dumped Caitlin Hart," Monica purred.

I was pretty sure I snarled at her.

"Where is that handsome fiancé of yours anyway?"

"In the kitchen helping out, but I'm afraid that's off-limits to everyone other than staff and tonight's volunteers. Now, if you'll excuse me, I have work to do." I turned and headed back to the bar, summoning every ounce of willpower I had not to deck the witch I'd been itching to punch it out with ever since she'd shown up on the island two weeks ago.

"What's she doing here?" Tara asked as I began refilling my tray with the next load of drinks.

"She's looking for Cody."

"Ask Finn to kick her out," Tara suggested. "You know she's only here to cause trouble."

I watched as the woman made her way around the bar, distributing her own sickeningly sweet brand of sensuality to every male, whether they were with a date or not. She stopped to smile at Chappy, kissed Pops on the cheek, then sat down across from Edwin, leaning in close, as if to have a serious conversation. I had to admit she knew how to use her God-given gifts.

I looked away from the woman who seemed to be working hard to piss me off and turned my attention to Tara. "Other than bumping into me, which I'm sure was intentional, she hasn't done anything to warrant removal from the premises. This is a public grand reopening and the whole community was invited. If I insist on her being bounced, I'll be the one who looks petty."

"She's on the island to steal your fiancé," Tara reminded me. "I don't think anyone would consider you petty for defending what's yours."

"I know why she's here and you know why she's here, but no one else other than family knows she's been threatening to seduce Cody away from me. Even Cody defended her in a roundabout way when I made it clear to him Monica was on the island for one reason and one reason only."

Tara frowned. "He defended her?"

"Sort of. First, he assured me that even if she *was* here to win him back, she had absolutely zero chance of success because I was the only one he'd ever loved or ever would love, but then he ruined his vow of devotion by adding that Monica had been drunk when Siobhan and I ran into her while dining at Antonio's, and he was sure she'd spoken out of turn when she made it clear she was on the island to rekindle things with him after all this time. He even hinted that perhaps I'd misunderstood what she said."

Tara picked up her tray. "Men are so clueless. They see a pretty face and a perfect body and their minds freeze up, preventing them from seeing the demon beneath the beauty." She added napkins. "I've no doubt Monica is here to do exactly what she threatened to do, but Cody loves you. I doubt he'll even notice if she comes on to him."

I hoped Tara was right, but I had my doubts. I remembered how Danny had followed Monica around like an obedient little puppy when they were dating, and he wasn't the type to trail any girl around. He was much more the love-'em-and-leave-'em sort, so the fact that she seemed to have mesmerized both Danny and Cody when she lived here before terrified me. I trusted Cody. I really did. It was Witch Monica I didn't trust.

"The group at table seven wants another round," Stacy informed me. She was a single mom with two-year-old twins who had recently moved to the island, a hard worker who seemed like a genuinely nice person. It was my opinion she would fit in to the O'Malley's family quite nicely.

"I'm on my way," I answered with a smile. "I think we're all going to be exhausted by the end of the evening, but I'm loving this turnout."

Stacy smiled back. "Yeah. I think the guys are pretty happy too." She picked up her own tray. "By the way, I saw what happened. I have your back if you need some help with the she-devil."

"Thanks. I appreciate the offer, but I can handle Monica if need be."

The next two hours were so crazy busy, I had little time to worry about, or keep track of, Monica. Finn was called away from his post by the door after an accident was reported on the highway. Of course this was Madrona Island, so a bouncer was probably unnecessary anyway.

By the time ten o'clock rolled around, the bar was so crowded it was almost impossible to walk through. I wasn't sure how Danny and Aiden were keeping up with the drink orders until I noticed Siobhan had joined them behind the bar. "Who's helping Cassie in the kitchen?" I asked my older sister.

"The brothers decided to close the kitchen and focus all their energy on the bar until closing. Aiden ordered a bunch of pizzas from the place down the street and Cassie went to pick them up. She's going to cut them into small pieces and we'll serve them as complimentary appetizers."

"That's a good idea." I looked around the room but didn't see Cody. "Did Cody go with her?"

Siobhan shook her head. "I don't think so. I'm not sure where he went. He was talking to Alex Turner, who showed up with Willow earlier, but I think they left to pick up the baby from his grandpa's."

Alex Turner and Willow Wood were friends who were co-parenting Willow's son, Barrington Wood Turner. Alex had adopted baby Barrington, who was named for his biological father, which made him legally responsible for him along with his mother, despite the fact that he and Willow weren't married or even dating. At least, they weren't dating in the traditional sense of the word. They were living together and raising a child, but so far their personal relationship seemed to have remained platonic.

By the time I'd delivered another round of drinks, things were beginning to clear out. Aiden and Danny planned to stay open until midnight if the bar was still hopping, but I was exhausted and hoped the party would break up earlier so I could head home and fall into what I was sure would be a dreamless sleep. Siobhan had left shortly after we spoke to pick up baby Connor from our mother's place. Connor was born to Finn and Siobhan just four months ago, but already it seemed most family events revolved around the totally adorable baby boy who looked just like his mama with the exception of his eyes, which were Finn all the way.

I'd set down my tray and was about to go outside to look for Cody when someone shoved me from behind, sending me into a table that tipped over, landing on top of me as my butt hit the floor. "What the—?" I was about to finish the sentence with a very unladylike four-letter word when I saw Monica smiling smugly at me. I'm not really sure what happened next; I guess my pent-up frustration with her finally got to me, because the next thing I knew, I was on my feet, and Monica was on her knees with her right arm pinned firmly behind her back.

"You witch," Monica screamed at the top of her lungs. "Are you insane? Let me go!"

I hesitated.

"Let her go, Cait." Danny walked up next to me.

"She started it."

"I didn't start anything, you raving lunatic. Now let me go or I'll have you arrested for assault."

Danny put his hand on mine. "It's okay. I saw what happened. I'll take care of it."

I released my grip and took a step back. Monica slapped me and called me a pathetic loser, which resulted in Danny grabbing her by the arm and dragging her away.

"Are you okay?" Aiden asked after Danny and Monica headed toward the back hallway.

I rubbed my cheek. "I'm okay. I just need some air. I'll be outside for a few minutes."

I left through the new side door onto the patio, where outdoor fire pits had been set up to provide warmth on cool evenings, and sat down on an empty bench. I wanted to cry, or yell, or even slap Monica back, but all I could manage was a few deep breaths to get myself under control. I hoped Danny would have shown Monica the door by the time I went back inside. The thin thread of patience I'd been clinging to since she'd returned to the island had definitely snapped when she'd thrown me into the table. Damn, that and the slap had hurt.

After a few minutes, Cody came out and sat down beside me. "Are you okay? I heard what happened."

"I'm okay. I just needed to get away. Where were you?"

"Out in the parking lot, talking to a couple of the guys from the softball team. I wasn't gone long. I needed some air after spending the entire evening in the kitchen." Cody put his arm around me and pulled me close. "Maybe I should take you home."

"No, I'm fine. I want to help with the cleanup, and the last thing I want to do is give Monica a reason to think she ran me off. That woman needs to go."

"I don't disagree, but I can't make her leave the island. I've told her that I'm not interested in what she's offering and I'm doing my best to avoid her, but I'm not sure what more I can do."

"People turn up missing all the time. No one knows why."

Cody raised a brow. "Really? You want me to dump her in the ocean?"

I shrugged. "I've had worse ideas."

Cody chuckled. "You're right. You have had worse ideas. But in this case, I think we might want to come up with a different strategy."

I huffed out a breath in frustration. "What strategy?"

"We could get married."

Now it was my turn to raise a brow. "Really? You want us to throw together a quickie wedding so your ex will leave us alone?"

"We've been engaged for a year," Cody pointed out in what seemed to be a much more serious tone than the one he'd used when we were discussing the option of a cement-boots burial.

I paused and then answered. "I know. And I want to marry you. But I'm not going to hurry things along just to get rid of Monica. We'll get married when we're ready to and not a minute before."

Cody put his hand to my cheek and turned me to look at him. "Just so you know, I'm ready."

I let out a long breath. "I know. But we have that one pesky problem I can't seem to find an answer for.

And no, I'm not referring to Monica. I'm referring to your mother."

Cody's mother was insisting that he and I get married in Florida, which was where she and several other West family members had moved after leaving Madrona Island. I wanted to get married on the island where I'd lived my entire life, with my family and friends. I wanted to get married in the church I'd attended since birth and I wanted to have the reception on the peninsula where I lived, down the beach from the house Cody would someday inherit and where we would raise our family.

"I told you, we can get married wherever you want," Cody countered.

"I know, but I don't want to start my married life with my mother-in-law hating me. I need another option."

"If I can work it out so my mom is happy and we're able to get married on Madrona Island, would you be willing to set a date?"

I nodded. "In a heartbeat."

Cody leaned in and kissed me lightly on the lips. "Okay. Let me see what I can work out with her. She can be stubborn, but in the end, she wants me to be happy."

"Okay," I said. "If you can work it out, we'll set a date." I leaned forward and kissed Cody slightly harder than he'd kissed me. "In the meantime, I think it's important we continue to practice for the honeymoon. Let's go in and start cleaning up. I have a bottle of wine and two glasses waiting for us back at the cabin."

Cody took my hand and pulled me to my feet. When we arrived inside, there were only a few partygoers still mingling around. One of Cody's friends had consumed way too much alcohol to be driving, so Cody ran him home, while Cassie, Tara, and I began cleaning up. By the time we'd cleared the empty glasses from the front and headed to the kitchen to start the cleanup in there, everyone had left with the exception of the two full-time waitresses and the family who'd stayed behind to help.

"I don't suppose anyone knows what happened to the mop?" I asked the rest of the cleaning crew.

"I think it might be in the storage room," Tara answered.

"Okay, I'll get it." I figured if we hurried with the cleanup, I could leave without feeling guilty once Cody returned. It had been a long night and I was beyond tired. Still, I was happy the evening had been a success. Other than the intrusion of Monica, it otherwise had been close to perfect. It seemed everyone on the island had come out to wish the brothers well, which I hoped indicated their venture would turn out to be even more successful than they'd hoped.

I stepped into the back hallway, which provided access to the back door and emergency access outside the building but was locked to prevent anyone sneaking inside. In addition, the hallway led to the business office, the men's and women's bathrooms, and the storage room. The office was supposed to be locked when Aiden, who handled the business end of things, wasn't working. While the brothers didn't have a lot of expensive equipment, the office did house a fairly new computer plus the safe, where change for the cash drawer was kept.

I walked past the bathrooms and opened the door to the storage room. It was dark, so I turned on the overhead light. A quick scan of the room revealed the mop, leaning against the back wall. The bucket was nearby, as was a broom and dustpan. I took several steps forward and was about to step over a tarp that had been tossed over something when I realized the object that was sticking out just a bit from the bottom of it was a human foot.

******

"Okay, walk me though everything that happened after I left to respond to the accident," Ryan Finnegan, the island resident deputy as well as my brother-in-law, asked after I'd called him to return to the bar.

I took a deep breath and thought about Danny before I answered. The first thing Finn had done after arriving was to separate everyone left on the premises. He was interviewing us each separately, and I knew I had to tell the truth, but no matter how I spun this, it wasn't going to look good for my younger brother. "Monica and I got into a fight," I began. "She started it and I guess she ended it too, but I did manage to bring her to her knees at one point."

"So it was a physical altercation?"

I nodded. "She bumped into me and knocked me to the floor. Once I managed to push the table that had fallen on top of me to the side, I jumped up and pulled her arm behind her back. I learned that in my self-defense class, and it brought her to her knees. She started screaming like I was killing her or something. Danny came over and told me to let her go, which I did grudgingly. I released her and she stood up and slapped me, and Danny grabbed her arm and pulled her toward the hallway."

"And after that?"

"I don't know. I didn't see her again. I assume Danny gave her a stern talking-to, then sent her out the back door to avoid another scene."

"That's exactly what Danny said happened," Finn confirmed. "Did the two of you discuss your response?"

I glared at Finn. "Really? Do you actually think this was some sort of an elaborate cover-up to get Monica out of my hair permanently?"

Finn lowered his notepad. "I don't think Danny killed Monica. And I don't think the two of you were part of some plot. But a woman is dead and you just admitted that Danny pulled her into the hallway, which was the last you saw of her."

"I know how it looks, but you have to believe Danny is telling you the truth. If he said he showed Monica to the back door, he did."

"So how did she get back in? The back door automatically locks when it's closed, which allows one-way access out of the building but not inside. I haven't had a chance to interview everyone who was here, but I called Tripp, who offered to keep an eye on the front door after I was called away, and he didn't remember Monica coming back in through the front door after Danny hauled her away." Tripp Brimmer had been the deputy for Madrona Island prior to his retirement.

I leaned back in my chair and let out a groan. "I know how it looks," I repeated, "but the bathrooms are down that hallway. A lot of people used them during the evening. The back door opens from the inside because it's a fire exit. Even if Monica didn't come back in through the front door, anyone could have opened the back door and let her back in once Danny tossed her out. All she had to do was text someone inside to help her."

"I suppose that's true, but so far, no one I've spoken to remembers seeing her after Danny hauled her away. If she came back in, why didn't she return to the party?"

"Maybe whoever let her in is the one who killed her. We both know she was a loose cannon. I'm sure she made a lot of enemies, years ago and since she's been back. I'm sure we're going to come up with a long list of people who had motive to want her out of their lives, including me, and no, I didn't do it."

"I agree she made a lot of enemies. And I agree we'll eventually come up with a long list of possible suspects who could have let her back in and then killed her. However, given the fact that Danny is the prime suspect at this point, and he's my brother-in-law, the sheriff is sending someone over from San Juan Island. Mitch Bronson will take over the investigation into Monica's death."

"Mitch? Mitch hates Danny."

"He has reason to dislike him after Danny had an affair with Mitch's ex, but he's convinced the sheriff he's over his ex and the entire incident with Danny is in the past. He convinced the sheriff he's able to be impartial, and apparently, the sheriff believed him. Given that Mitch used to live on Madrona Island, the sheriff realizes he has relationships with the individuals who'll serve as witnesses. I'm not saying I agree, but the sheriff has decided Mitch is a good person to take over. There wasn't a thing I could say to change his mind."

Chapter 2

Saturday, October 27

Cody and I talked about the situation late into the night. We both struggled with the question of who had killed Monica, but I struggled even more over my guilt that a part of me was almost glad she was dead. I didn't want to be that person: someone who would find happiness in the death of another. I knew it was wrong and I knew that finding joy in the misfortune of others was a dark and slippery slope to travel. Maybe I should talk to Father Bartholomew about it when I was next at the church. He seemed like the sort to have stored away a lot of good advice to share with his flock when necessary, and I felt like I needed any advice he could give me.

Coffee Cat Books was open on Saturdays and I really needed to get to work on time. Saturday was usually the busiest day of the week, so Tara and I tried to arrive early to get everything ready for the first ferry. What I really wanted to do was work on

Monica's murder investigation because I was sure Mitch would be gunning for Danny, but I had other responsibilities to see to, so investigating would have to wait. Cody was caught up at the newspaper, so he planned to head over to Aiden's to talk to both my brothers. The previous evening, they had still been sequestered, awaiting the arrival of Deputy Bronson, when Cody and I were sent on our way, so we hadn't had a chance to speak to them to find out what, if anything, they knew.

Cody and I arranged to meet for lunch. I hoped by then he would have an update on the status of the investigation. We'd discussed inviting the entire sleuthing team over that evening if Mitch hadn't eliminated Danny as a suspect by then.

"I have a soy latte and two white mochas for Beverly," I called out, setting all three drinks on the counter.

Coffee Cat Books was a bookstore that also featured a coffee bar and a cat lounge. Tara and I owned the enterprise, while Willow and Cassie worked for us part time. Cassie was attending college in Seattle and so was only home on weekends, but I could sense she hadn't been as enthralled with college life as she'd hoped, so I was half-expecting her to come back to the island for good after the semester break. Personally, I hoped she'd stick it out. I hadn't gone to college, so I wasn't one to talk, but Cassie was a bright girl who could do anything she wanted with a good education.

"I also had a blueberry muffin and a chocolate scone," the girl picking up the drinks informed me.

"Hang on. I'll get them." I'd turned around to the pastry counter to bag the baked goods when I noticed

Mitch Bronson lingering near the used-book shelves. He didn't seem to be checking out the stock; he looked a lot more interested in the people in the store. I glanced at Tara, who was busy chatting with a couple from Portland. I wasn't sure she'd even noticed our visitor yet. "Here you go." I gave the woman the items she'd indicated she'd ordered.

"I bet that cop is here to ask about the lady who died in the bar last night," the woman whose order I'd just filled whispered to me.

"So you heard about that…"

"Better. I was there."

I narrowed my gaze and looked more closely at her. She didn't look familiar. I was pretty sure she didn't live on the island but decided to ask anyway. "Do you live on Madrona?"

"No. My friend Polly and I are here from Spokane for the weekend. We noticed the bar was hopping when we drove by, so we decided to check it out."

"I don't remember seeing you."

"We arrived late, but we managed to get a table on the deck, which, by the way, is really cozy and welcoming. We didn't stay all that long. We had one drink and were just about to leave when we met these two guys who asked us if we wanted to get some food. We rode with them to a restaurant, and when they brought us back to the bar to get our car, we noticed the cops were there. We met a guy in the parking lot who told us what happened."

"What guy? In the parking lot? What guy?"

The woman shrugged. "Just some guy. Tall. Blond. Maybe thirty. I didn't pay that much attention. To be honest, I'd had a few by then and was more interested in getting back to the motel before any more cops showed up. The last thing I need is another DUI."

"Did you notice anyone else loitering in the parking lot when you went to get your car?" I asked.

The woman tilted her head. "I don't think so. It was just the one guy. I noticed the cop car and maybe three or four other vehicles in the lot. The guy I spoke to said there was just one cop inside, along with the owners of the bar and a handful of employees. I guess most of the real excitement was over by then." She looked toward her friend. "I gotta go. Nice chatting with you."

What guy? I asked myself again.

After I'd found Monica's body in the storage room, I'd told Aiden and Danny, who'd called Finn. We'd checked to make sure both the front and back doors were locked while we waited. Siobhan had gone home, as had all the customers, which just left Aiden and Danny, Stacy and Libby, Tara, Cassie, and me, when I found the body. Cody had come back from driving his friend home shortly after.

Once Finn arrived, he'd removed the tarp from atop the body to reveal the fact that someone had hit Monica on the back of the head with a heavy object. A search of the room revealed that the object had most likely been removed from the premises by the killer; nothing Finn found matched the wound. Of course, the crime scene guys would come over from the county office and do a much more thorough investigation.

Whether the murder weapon was found later or not was irrelevant to what I considered to be the question of the day: How did some random guy who was loitering in the parking lot know that a woman had been found dead in the bar? He might have seen Finn's car and suspected something was up, although everyone knew Finn was related by marriage to Danny and Aiden, so even that wasn't a foregone conclusion. But even if he did suspect Finn was at the bar in an official capacity, how could he possibly have known a woman had been found dead? The only people who knew about the murder right then were inside the bar. Unless the guy was the killer...

"I need to call Finn," I said to Tara. "I know it's busy, but it's important. I'll hurry."

Tara gave me a meaningful glance, but I couldn't fill her in with a coffee bar full of customers within hearing distance, so I simply handed her my drink list and headed for the office. Hopefully, Finn would be in and able to take my call.

******

As it turned out, Finn had been taken off the case completely, as he'd suspected he would be, but I still told him about the tall blond man in the parking lot, who somehow knew a woman had been murdered, despite the fact that no one other than the handful of people inside the bar should have known that yet. Finn agreed that seemed significant and promised to come over so we could discuss it in more depth. Fortunately, the woman who'd provided the tip had paid for her drinks and treats with a credit card, so he should be able to track her down to get a more detailed description of the man she'd seen.

Cody had spent the morning with Danny and Aiden, who hadn't come up with any explanation for what could have happened. Danny swore he gave

Monica a good scolding for slapping me, then sent her on her way via the back door. Aiden said he'd been so busy he was barely even aware of what was going on until someone filled him in later.

We all decided to meet for dinner to try to come up with a plan of action that wouldn't land us all in jail. It certainly made it trickier when Finn wasn't the deputy in charge of an investigation, but just because it was tricky didn't mean it was impossible. In addition to Finn and Siobhan and Danny and Aiden, Cody and I invited Tara. Cassie was staying with Finn and Siobhan and would most likely be around too.

We chose to gather at Finn and Siobhan's. They lived in the house that once belonged to our aunt Maggie directly behind my cabin, so they could put Connor to bed when the time came. Siobhan offered to make dinner for everyone because she was off for the weekend from her job as mayor. Cody offered to bring some beverages, and I suggested we pick up some dessert as well.

Over lunch, Cody and I were sitting in a booth at the back of the restaurant, so I was able to speak freely, telling him about my conversation with the woman at the bookstore.

"It does seem odd that someone who wasn't in the bar would know what was going on inside," Cody agreed. "Are you sure no one else was around when you found the body?"

"I'm sure. You'd gone to take your friend home. Danny and Aiden were cleaning up in the front, and Libby and Stacy were washing glasses, while Tara, Cassie, and I were cleaning up in the kitchen. I went into the storage room to find the mop and almost stumbled over Monica's body. I was startled but didn't scream or do anything that would have alerted anyone outside to the fact that we had a problem. I went out front and told Danny and Aiden what I'd found. Aiden locked the front door while Danny called Finn. You showed up a few minutes after that, and the door was locked when you arrived."

"It was," Cody agreed. "I texted you to let you know I was back and asked you to let me in. And I do remember seeing only you, Danny, Aiden, Stacy, Libby, Tara, and Cassie at the time. Finn showed up a few minutes after I did."

"So it seems unlikely news of the murder could somehow have left the bar."

Cody nodded. "Yes, that seems to be the case."

"So the tall blond guy has to be the killer. Right?"

Cody paused. "It would make it easy if he were, but there are other ways to explain how he might have known what was going on. Danny escorted Monica to the back hallway when things were in full swing. It's possible he could have opened the wrong door looking for the bathroom and seen the body."

"Then why didn't he report it? Why didn't he call the cops? Why didn't he do something?"

"Maybe he was frightened. Maybe he has a police record, or maybe he just didn't want to get involved. When he saw Finn's car in the lot, he could have figured the body had been found and then made the comment he did to the women when they came for their car."

I scrunched up my face. "Maybe. I suppose that's a plausible explanation, but it seems sort of far-fetched to me."

"Perhaps. We can discuss it with the others this evening. Maybe someone else has a better idea of how he could have known what he did."

******

When Cody and I arrived at Finn and Siobhan's, I was amazed to find she'd decorated for Halloween. She hadn't had anything up the last time I'd been there, a couple of days before.

"Wow, the place looks great. When did you do all this?" I asked my sister.

"This afternoon. I had the lights and garland tucked away in a box. Finn brought home the pumpkins. I'd given up on the idea of decorating this year, with Halloween just a few days away, but I had some time while Connor was napping and I suddenly felt motivated to make the effort because everyone was coming by this evening."

I ran my hand along the edge of the mantel, which looked very festive with candles, orange lights, and colorful fall leaves. "Well, it looks fantastic. Now I wish I'd made the effort myself, but I don't think I'll have time to get to it."

"You have two days off," Siobhan pointed out.

"I know, but I have a feeling unless Mitch has come up with something, Cody and I are going to be spending the rest of the weekend trying to figure out who killed Monica."

Siobhan set a large tray with cheese and crackers on the table near several types of spread I guessed were the appetizers for the evening. "Speaking of the investigation, don't you think a cat should have shown up by now?"

Siobhan had a point. In the past, one of the island's magical cats always showed up to help me solve mysteries. It was true we'd had an issue with the cats leaving the island months ago, but Cody and I had dealt with that issue while we were in New Orleans in the summer. At least, I'd thought we had. This was the first murder on Madrona Island since my witch friend Tansy and I had made the trip into the hollow to right the imbalance and restore the magic.

"That's a good question. I can't believe I haven't wondered the same thing. Maybe I should call Tansy. It does seem odd that a cat hasn't arrived by now." I looked out Siobhan's kitchen door toward my cabin. "You haven't seen a cat hanging around today, have you?"

"No, although I haven't been out in the yard all that much today. Cassie went over to the cat sanctuary this morning before she left for the bookstore to feed the cats and see to the cleaning. I was going to head over in a while to take care of the second feeding of the day, but I haven't had the chance yet."

"I'll go," I offered. "I'll call Tansy while I'm there."

The Harthaven Cat Sanctuary was the brainchild of my aunt Maggie to provide a safe haven for the island's feral cats. The sanctuary, which was built on the property she owned and on which we both lived, housed both long-term residents and temporary ones waiting for adoption. Before Maggie moved off the island, she and I had taken responsibility for the care of the cats together. Now Siobhan and I shared the duties, although Cassie pitched in quite a lot when she was on the island.

Four years ago, I'd met my first magical cat. Romeo had helped me solve the death of a man from the island council and had since gone to live with my neighbor, Francine Rivers, and her cat, Juliet. Since then, I'd partnered with more than a dozen cats to solve murders and other mysteries that continually found their way into my path. The fact that there had been a murder the night before yet no cat had shown up was fairly alarming, given everything else that had been going on with the cats and the magic on the island in general.

I called Tansy while I walked across the lawn to the sanctuary, but she didn't answer, so I left a detailed message and asked her to call me back. I just hoped she was on the island. It wasn't unusual at all for Tansy to ditch her phone and all forms of communication and technology to go on retreat for a few days. I supposed I couldn't blame her. In addition to being a witch, she had both the ability and the burden of knowing the future and having to decide what to do about it. I couldn't imagine how traumatic it would be to know something bad was going to happen but to also realize it wasn't your destiny to do anything to prevent it.

Still, Tansy did intervene at times, and that was usually where the magical cats and I came in.

"So, how are we all doing today?" I asked the cats as I entered the sanctuary. It was divided into several rooms. There was one for socially adjusted cats who were waiting for me to find them a forever home, one for less well-adjusted permanent residents, one for mama cats and their babies, and even one for cats that needed to be isolated for one reason or another.

In the main space, where most of the cats hung out, several crossed the room to greet me, including our newest resident, who'd never done that before. I bent over and picked up the black-and-brown-spotted cat that looked like a small leopard. He'd been brought to us by a motorist who'd found him injured on the side of the road more than a month ago. Mystic was an ornery sort who wasn't one to cuddle, but that was what he seemed to want to do today, a completely new behavior for him. I hoped this indicated he'd eventually make a good pet for someone. My wish for all the cats in my care was that they'd find a warm and loving forever home.

Once everyone was fed and played with, I went back to the house. The others had all shown up and Siobhan had set up a murder board. Someone had filled in some basic information, such as the name of the victim and current suspects. The fact that Danny's name was on the board was disturbing, but he was only there as a reminder that we needed to find a way to clear his name, not because any of us believed he'd actually done it.

"Dinner will be ready in thirty minutes," Siobhan announced. "I'm fine with starting the conversation, but I worked hard on my casserole, so when it's ready, we're all taking a break to eat it."

Naturally, we all agreed.

"Is Mitch sharing any information with you?" I asked Finn.

"No. I figure if we can clear Danny, the sheriff will have no reason to keep me off the case," he answered, then looked at Danny. "You said you sent Monica on her way through the back door. Did anyone see you escort her out?"

Danny shook his head. "I don't think so. At least, I don't remember anyone being in the hallway when I dragged Monica out."

"Did she fight you when you grabbed her arm and dragged her to the back?" Finn asked.

"Actually, she tried to seduce me. It was sickening. The entire time I was yelling at her for slapping Cait, she was rubbing up against me and grabbing things she had no business grabbing. I know she'd been drinking, but I can't imagine what happened to her. She was such a sweet girl when we dated."

I rolled my eyes. She was a snake back then as well, but Danny just couldn't see it. I'd pretty much decided Monica's talent was hypnotizing men so they only saw what she wanted them to see. The woman had always been bad news.

"Okay, so you tossed her out the back door and then what?" Finn asked.

"I went back to the bar. It was busy, so I didn't have time to linger."

"How long were you away from the main part of the bar altogether?" Finn asked.

Danny shrugged. "A couple of minutes. I grabbed Monica and pulled her into the hallway. I tried to talk to her at first. I wanted her to understand her behavior wouldn't be tolerated and she wouldn't be welcome back. I tried to suggest she should leave the island before she ruined her reputation completely, but she was all hands, so I could see she wasn't really listening. I thought about dragging her back through the bar to the front door, but the way she was all over me, I just wanted her gone, so I opened the back door and gave her a little shove out. Then I closed the door and went back to the bar. I never saw her come back in, so I'm not sure how she ended up in the storage room."

"Cody and I thought maybe someone let her back in through the same door you used to put her out," I offered. "It does open without a key from the inside."

"I guess if someone knew she was out there that would be a plausible explanation. If someone let her in, I don't think she ever made it back to the bar. Whoever let her in must have been the one to kill her." Danny looked at Finn. "Did Mitch take prints off the doorknob?"

"He did. The fact that he was willing to answer some of my questions today made me feel a little better about things. Anyway, one of the things he shared was that he tested the doorknob and there were a bunch of fingerprints, including yours."

Danny sighed. "Yeah, my prints would be in the mix."

"And mine," Aiden added.

"And mine," I said. "I let in the guy delivering the kegs through that door earlier in the day."

"And Edwin's," Tara added. "I noticed he used the back door to go out to grab a smoke when no one else was watching."

"Yeah, the back door has always been used for that purpose by some of the regulars," Aiden confirmed.

"So it sounds like unless we come across a set of prints that really shouldn't be there, they most likely won't help," Siobhan concluded.

"What about someone who might have been in one of the bathrooms?" Cassie asked. "Even if Danny didn't see them, they might have seen him."

"Or maybe heard Danny and Monica arguing," Tara added. "All we really need to find out to clear Danny is someone who saw or heard Danny escort Monica out."

Building on that, I added, "Or maybe someone saw a person other than Danny let her back in."

"We need a list of everyone we remember being in the bar," Cody concluded. "Once we have that we can split it up and start talking to people. Someone must have seen or heard something."

There were so many people in and out of the bar last night that talking to everyone seemed daunting, yet I didn't have a better idea. I filled the others in on the tall blond man who'd been seen in the parking lot and seemed to know about the murder before it was made public knowledge, and then Siobhan called a break while dinner was served. Cassie and Tara went to help her set out the food while I tried calling Tansy again. When she still didn't answer, I tried her business and life partner, Bella, who did.

"Oh Cait. I'm so sorry," Bella said after I explained there'd been a murder and I needed her help. "Tansy's on retreat. She left several days ago, though she did tell me that you'd be calling. I have a message for you."

"Okay. I'm listening."

"She said you should work with the spotted newcomer who most recently greeted you."

At first I had no idea who that could be, but then I remembered Mystic. The idea that Tansy would know before she left that there would be a murder and I would need a cat was beyond comprehension. For her to know I would call Bella and get the message shortly after being greeted by Mystic seemed downright impossible.

Chapter 3

Sunday, October 28

The previous evening we came up with a list of people to speak to and divided it between us. The list was extensive, and covering all of it would take forever. We'd started with the individuals who seemed most likely to have a reason to want Monica dead. After a bit of back and forth, Cody and I had six suspects to track down and talk to today. Of them, two attended St. Patrick's Catholic Church, where Cody and I volunteered with the children's choir.

After receiving Tansy's message from Bella, I decided to bring Mystic to my cabin. If I understood Tansy correctly, it seemed he was going to be the cat who'd come to help me, and I wanted to be sure he was close by. In addition to Cody, Mystic, and me, my dog Max was also in residence in my cabin. Cody was sleeping in this morning, so I grabbed Max, pulled on my running shoes, and headed to the beach that lined the property.

Running along the waterline in the early morning is one of my very favorite things to do. I love the way the sky turns from black to gray and eventually, if I'm lucky, to pink, red, and sometimes even orange. I love to run across the sand as the first eagles and seagulls of the day show up in search of a meal. I love the gentle breeze that blows in from the west, and the rolling waves as they fold themselves onto the sandy beach. I love the smell of salt in the air and the song of the birds who call the seashore their home. I love everything about Madrona Island. It's been my home my entire life and I can't imagine a situation in which it wouldn't continue to be until the day I die.

As I jogged lazily behind Max, I thought of the six people Cody and I'd be speaking with today. Tim Pierson was also a member of St. Patrick's and had two children, Tammy and Tim Junior, who participated in the children's choir. Tim was married to Patty, a lifelong islander who'd been in the same graduating class as Cody, Danny, and Monica. She was credited with stealing away the captain of the football team, a senior at the time, from Monica. Patty had scored a huge boost on the social scene for landing him when she was still a junior, achieving bonus status points for the steal.

So how would that make Tim a suspect? From what Danny had heard, Monica wasn't the sort to let go of an old grudge, and after returning to the island, she'd made up her mind to get back at Patty by sharing a juicy piece of gossip that was guaranteed to totally upend the happy life she'd built. Danny wasn't sure why she believed Monica, but apparently, when she told Patty she'd seen Tim coming out of a local motel with another woman, Patty had been heartbroken and had left the island to stay with her sister. In Danny's opinion, Tim was as much a victim of Monica's cruel act of revenge as Patty. I supposed it made sense Tim would be outraged after what had happened, but in my mind, for Patty to so easily believe her husband had been unfaithful to her probably meant she already had her suspicions.

Still, Tim had been at the bar on Friday night, and he was a regular, so he knew about the back door and the storage room. Tim had consumed more alcohol than was probably wise, which could very well have led to impaired judgment. Danny also had said Tim had been overheard threatening to put an end to the witch who was going around the island spreading lies.

The second person Cody and I were supposed to speak with was a Madrona Island resident and parishioner at St. Pat's, Nancy Dalton. She'd been dating a local, Eric Libertine. Actually, I was pretty sure she'd moved here in the first place to be near Eric. According to what Siobhan shared, Nancy had felt things were moving along well with him. She was even beginning to hint at an engagement in the future until he blew off a date with her to spend the evening with Monica.

Like Tim, Nancy had been at the bar on Friday, and they were two of the last to leave. She'd been drinking, although none of us knew if she was aware of the storage room or the back door. Still, if she had used the ladies' room, she could have seen both.

In addition to the two suspects Cody and I were likely to run into at church, we had four others to track down. All had motive and had been at the bar that night. It was too soon to try to figure out which, if any, of our six might turn out to be the killer, but Monica had been such an unpleasant person, it could have been any of them.

Cody was up and about by the time Max and I returned from our run. I jumped in the shower while he made us some breakfast. It was nice to be part of a couple. Before getting together with Cody, I'd enjoyed living alone, but now the mornings when he wasn't around felt empty and lonely.

As I washed my hair, I thought about the fact that Cody was ready to set a date for our wedding, while I was still stalling. As I'd told him, my not being in a hurry had nothing to do with not wanting to marry him and everything to do with not wanting a conflict with his mother. I hoped he really could work out a compromise that would make everyone happy. Of course, once we exchanged our vows, it made sense for me to give up the cabin and move in with Cody in the house he lived in with my neighbor, Mr. Parsons. I totally understood and agreed with Cody that he shouldn't live alone at his age, but I sure would miss the little place that had been such a big part of my life for so many years.

I supposed I could pass it along to Cassie, who would have her own place to stay when she was home from college and wouldn't have to worry about paying rent, and if she did decide to drop out and return to the island full time, which I suspected she might, she might not want to live with our mother.

I closed my eyes as the warm water ran over my head to rinse the shampoo from my hair. Living at Mr. Parsons's wouldn't be so bad. His estate was right down the beach from my cabin, like the rest of the Hart property. Cody helped to take care of Mr. Parsons, who now lived on the first floor of his large home, and had his own apartment on the third floor, which he'd tried very hard to make as comfortable for me as possible. And it was a lovely home. It just wasn't *my* home.

Change was a part of life, and I knew if I wanted a life with Cody—and I did—I needed to find a way to get past everything that was holding me back and make the commitment that ultimately I knew I would, sooner or later.

Cody had breakfast ready by the time I joined him in the kitchen and eating area.

"I think there's something wrong with this cat," Cody said after pouring me a cup of coffee.

"Why? Do you think he's trying to provide us with a clue?"

"No," Cody said. "Not a clue. I'm thinking a hair ball. He keeps hacking like he's going to upchuck, but then he doesn't."

I squatted down on the floor next to Mystic. "Are you okay, sweetie?"

The cat began to purr as I ran my hands over him. "He seems okay now."

Cody shrugged. "Maybe, but you might want to keep an eye on him. Do you want toast with your eggs?"

"Yes, please."

We sat down at the dining table, which was situated in front of a window that overlooked the sea. It was such a beautiful morning. I was sorry the entire day promised to be focused on murder, betrayal, and Monica. It would be the perfect day for a long, leisurely hike, or maybe a drive around the island.

These warm autumn days would soon give way to the colder ones of winter, which made a beautiful day like today that much more precious.

******

"Fiona is supposed to sing the solo during the first set, but her mother called to say she has the flu," I told Cody as we were organizing the kids to go on for eleven o'clock Mass.

"Brianna knows the lyrics," Cody answered. "We discussed mixing it up so Brianna didn't dominate things, but in this case, I think she's our best choice."

"Agreed. I'll let her know about the change. While I'm doing that, remind the boys to sing louder. I feel like all that's coming through are female voices."

"I will." Cody glanced toward the door to the choir room. "Tim Pierson is dropping off his kids. Why don't you pull him aside while you have the opportunity, and I'll talk to Brianna?"

"Are you sure? He might be more apt to talk to another guy."

Cody handed me his clipboard. "I'll talk to him while you organize the kids."

I frowned as I accepted the clipboard. Although I'd been the one to suggest Cody talk to Tim, he'd gotten the better end of the deal.

"Okay, let's settle down," I yelled loud enough to get everyone's attention. "We have a few changes we need to go over, and I need to make sure you're all listening." I looked around the room. "Does anyone know where Ricky and Robby went? They were just here a few minutes ago."

"They went to the bathroom," one of the other boys said.

"Well, that can't be good," I mumbled under my breath. Ricky and Robby were awesome kids, but they both had high energy levels and shared the tendency to make trouble if given the opportunity. I just hoped they weren't clogging all the toilets, which they'd done the last time they'd been in the bathroom together.

By the time I'd gone over all the changes to the day's program, Cody had returned. Ricky and Robby filed in a few minutes later. Cody took charge of getting everyone lined up to file into the church and I took up the rear, to make sure no one escaped before we made it to our destination. Leading the children's choir certainly had been a learning experience for me. Prior to taking on the obligation, I'd had no idea how downright sneaky kids could be.

As we filed in through the front door of the church, I spotted Nancy Dalton near the coffee cart. I motioned to Cody that I was going over to talk to her as he got everyone situated on the three-tier bleachers. Cody nodded, indicating he'd received my silent message.

"Hey, Nancy," I greeted her.

"Hey, Cait. I hope you aren't here for coffee. We shut things down five minutes before the start of Mass."

"No, I'm not here for coffee. I just wanted to talk to you for a minute. Can we step outside?"

Nancy looked uncertain.

"It'll be quick, I promise. It's about Monica Caldron."

Nancy's lips tightened. "What did she do now? Seduce the pope?"

"No, nothing quite that extreme. But there's been a development. Let's go out onto the front steps and I'll fill you in."

When I told Nancy that Monica was dead, she looked legitimately shocked. So shocked, in fact, that she pretty much convinced me that she couldn't have been the one to kill her. "I noticed you were at the bar on Friday night when she slapped me and Danny hauled her away. I wondered if you noticed anything that might help us determine what happened to her."

Nancy paused. "I don't know. I remember her slapping you after you put her on her knees, and Danny saying something to both of you. I remember hoping he was kicking her out when he hauled her into the back. I guess he must have, because he came back alone. I don't remember seeing her at all after that."

"Did you see anyone else head toward the hallway?"

"Sure. Lots of people. The bathrooms are down that hall, and there was a whole lot of beer being consumed that night."

"Did you see anyone go into or come out of the hallway after Danny and Monica went that way but before Danny came back?"

"Conrad Roundtree. I was curious to see what he was going to do. The woman was such a total witch. I hoped she wasn't going to come back to the party. Anyway, I had my eye on the hallway so I could see who would return. I noticed Conrad Roundtree came back from the hallway before Danny did. I guess he must have been in the bathroom."

I smiled. "Great. That really helps." Hopefully, Conrad had seen Danny escorting Monica out the back door, which should help to clear him from Mitch Bronson's suspect list.

******

"Tim seemed genuinely shocked to hear Monica was dead," Cody informed me after Mass and we'd sent the kids back to their parents. We'd stayed behind to tidy up the choir room. "I don't think he's our guy, although he did admit that Monica told Patty the truth when she said she saw him coming out of a motel with another woman. He had been having an affair but was feeling bad about it and planned to break it off if Monica hadn't let the cat out of the bag."

"So maybe Monica actually did Patty a favor," I said.

Cody shrugged. "Maybe. In a roundabout way, Tim provided an alibi for one of the other suspects on our list. It seems he was sitting with Don Jones, one of the men Monica dated and dumped in the two weeks she was back. Anyway, according to Tim, he and Don were chatting about football scores when Danny hauled Monica into the back room, and they continued to chat until they both left the bar at around eleven o'clock. Tim mentioned Don as an alibi for himself, so if Don says the same thing, that would clear him as well, and that would leave us with only three people to track down this afternoon: Lacy Goodman, Adam Goldberg, and Kent Collins."

"Four, actually. Nancy saw Conrad Roundtree come out of the hallway after Danny and Monica went down there but before Danny returned. I'm hoping he either saw or overheard whatever happened after Danny hauled Monica away from the party. I'm pretty sure he works over at the Harthaven Marina on the weekends. We should stop by to chat with him."

"Lacy Goodman works in the little market right near there," Cody commented. "Let's head home and change our clothes. We can pick up Max and check on Mystic, then see if we can touch base with everyone we're supposed to follow up with."

Back at the cabin, Cody and I changed out of our church clothes and into jeans and sweatshirts. Then we made sandwiches so we didn't have to stop for lunch. I took Max out for a quick bathroom break while Cody tossed together a fruit salad to go with the ham and cheese sandwiches. By the time I returned, Cody was sitting on the floor holding Mystic.

"What's up?" I asked as I wiped the sand from Max's paws.

"The cat was doing that choking thing again. I think it's intentional, but I have no idea why he'd do it, and why he only does it when you aren't here."

"Maybe he's just trying to get your attention." I smiled at Cody, who was cradling Mystic. "It seems to work."

Cody looked less than certain as he set down the cat and stood up. "Maybe. But I'm not sure we should leave him here alone."

"We can bring him." I crossed the room to wash my hands. "Max too. Max will love the ride, and maybe Mystic will lead us to a clue along the way. Did you remember to use up those red grapes we bought at the farmers market?"

"They're in the salad," Cody confirmed as he washed his own hands.

"Okay, so let's talk strategy," I suggested as I dug into my lunch. I guess I was hungrier than I thought. "We'll start at the marina. Hopefully, Conrad and Lacy will both be working today. Of the others, two live to the north of the marina and one to the south. I'm not sure if we should just show up at people's homes or if we should call them to let them know we want to speak to them. I'd hate to tip off the guilty party, if one of the suspects on the list turns out to be the killer, but it seems rude to just show up at the home of a casual acquaintance on a Sunday."

"Let's start at the marina and figure it out from there." Cody picked up the list and looked at it. "I bet we'll be able to find Adam Goldberg at the bowling alley. Seems to me I saw a poster about a tournament this weekend."

"Okay. We'll just get started and see where we end up. If we're lucky, we'll identify the killer quickly so we don't even need to bother everyone on the list."

"And if Conrad can vouch for Danny, that will take a lot of pressure off us to wrap this up fast."

******

Unfortunately, things didn't work out quite the way we hoped. While Conrad *had* come out of the bathroom while Danny was in the hallway arguing with Monica, he hadn't seen him toss her out the door. What he had seen, it turned out, was Danny shaking Monica by the arm while he yelled at her for slapping me. According to Conrad, Danny was about as mad as he'd ever seen him, which made him feel somewhat afraid for her. He told Mitch Bronson he was thinking about sending someone after Danny when he reappeared and went back to the bar. Conrad's statement hadn't helped Danny in the least. If anything, it seemed to put another nail in his coffin.

I just hoped one of the others on our list would provide us with information that would counteract the image I was sure Mitch had already formed of what went on Friday night.

As we thought, Lacy Goodman did work in the little marina market, and she was there when we arrived. She had made it onto our suspect list because she was working evenings at one of the diners in town until Monica complained to her boss that she'd been rude to her, which got her fired. Cody and I knew Lacy pieced together a living working a lot of different jobs. Being fired from any of them was bound to hurt her financially.

"Yeah, I was at the bar on Friday, and yes, I remember Monica slapping Cait," Lacy said when Cody asked her. "If she'd slapped me, I would have slapped her back."

"Trust me, if Danny hadn't intervened, I would have," I replied. "We were wondering if you saw Danny escort her to the back hallway."

"Yeah. Pretty much everyone in the bar saw what happened. After she pushed you and the table fell on you, every eye in the place was trained on the scene as it unfolded. I hope Danny banned her for life. That woman is self-centered and egotistical and doesn't give a crap about who she hurts as long as she gets whatever it is she thinks she deserves."

"I think Danny did ban her, not that it matters now," I said. "I guess you haven't heard: Monica's dead."

Lacy's eyes grew big. "Monica was the woman who was found dead in the back room of the bar?"

"So you did hear," I said.

"I heard there was a body, but I didn't know it was Monica's. I guess I just assumed it was someone who drank too much and had a heart attack or something. I assume she didn't have a heart attack?"

"She was hit over the head with a blunt object," I replied.

"Well, I'll be. I guess karma is real after all."

I wasn't sure if someone being murdered—even someone as awful as Monica—would fall under the realm of karma, but I could understand why Lacy might feel that way. "I don't suppose you noticed if anyone went toward the hallway or emerged from it after Danny and Monica went that way but before Danny came back to the bar?"

Lacy shook her head. "I'm sorry. I wasn't paying attention. I went outside for a smoke with Kent Collins after I saw Danny walking off with Monica. Did you know Kent was almost kicked out of his apartment when Monica complained to the manager that he was too loud? Too loud? Kent? That guy is usually as quiet as a mouse. Kent told me what really happened. He got the parking spot she considered to be hers, even though it was assigned to him and she was only visiting and didn't even live in the building."

"Monica was staying in the apartment building where Kent lives?" One of the others had put Kent on the list because Monica had been harassing him, but I hadn't realized why until now.

"She was staying with Peter Fordman for a while, but I think she moved into a motel at some point. I don't think he was a Monica fan from the beginning. It seems Peter's sister asked him to let her use his spare room. If you ask me, he was a saint to put up with her for as long as he did. I know his sister was tight with Monica when they were in high school, and Peter would give you the shirt off his back, but dealing with Monica for even a few days would be above and beyond the call of duty."

I remembered Peter's sister. She'd left the island shortly after graduation. As far as I knew, she'd never been back, but it was possible she'd asked her older brother to let her old friend stay in his extra room while she was on Madrona. I wondered if Mitch had spoken to Peter yet.

"Did you notice anyone lingering by the back door of the bar when you and Kent were outside?"

"There were a couple of guys smoking and talking. I didn't pay much attention to them, so I can't give you their names. They went back inside before Kent and I did."

Cody and I spoke to Lacy for a while longer and then returned to the car. We hadn't brought the animals with us after all because we'd thought they'd have to spend too much time waiting in the car. We still needed to talk to Adam Goldberg, so we swung by the bowling alley, hoping he was there. Unfortunately, he wasn't, leaving us feeling as if we were batting zero for the day. Investigations took time, but things were looking really bad for Danny.

Chapter 4

When we got to my cabin I called Siobhan. Mitch Bronson was still mostly keeping Finn out of the loop, but it was his opinion that Mitch had found out something that gave him even more reason to suspect Danny of killing Monica. Finn went so far as to say his gut impression was that Mitch was putting his ducks in a row in preparation for making an arrest. But Finn had no idea what information Mitch had. I shared with Siobhan that Conrad had seen Danny yelling at Monica and had been concerned for her safety. We hoped that was all he had on Danny, but Finn thought he probably had more.

The question was, what more? Danny obviously hadn't killed the woman, so there shouldn't be any proof to find. Was someone setting him up? That was a possibility I'd keep in the back of my mind as we continued to investigate.

I decided it was time to see if Mystic had something to show me. So far, all he'd done was freak Cody out with his coughing. Of course, every time Mystic coughed, Cody dropped what he was doing and came running, so my suspicion was that we were dealing with a very smart cat who knew how to get attention when he wanted it.

I sat down on the floor and Mystic wandered over and head-butted me. For a cat who had all but ignored me up until yesterday, he certainly had developed an affectionate streak. "Okay, kitty," I said as I pulled him onto my lap. "We're looking for clues that will lead us to the person who killed Monica. According to the message Tansy left for me, it appears you're supposed to help with that. So, where do we start?"

Mystic rubbed his head against my cheek, then climbed out of my lap. He crossed the room and jumped up on the kitchen counter, where I'd left the remainder of the wine Cody and I had recently shared. He pawed at the bottle, which told me it was important.

"The bar," I said aloud. "You think we should go to the bar." I looked at Cody. "Is it still taped off?"

"I don't know. I'll call Finn to find out. If it isn't, I'll call Danny to see if he's home. He can let us in."

Danny lived in the apartment above the bar. The town of Harthaven, where O'Malley's was located, had a big Catholic population, so it had always been closed on Sundays. Danny and Aiden had discussed staying open seven days a week, but the island was heading into our slow season, so they were keeping to the Tuesday through Saturday schedule O'Malley had adhered to, at least for the time being.

Danny reported to Cody that he'd been staying with Aiden since Friday night. They were watching the football game, but if we wanted to take a look around in the bar, he'd meet us there to let us in. Mitch had called him to say he'd removed the yellow tape from the building earlier that morning and it was all right for him to go back to the apartment, but he and Aiden were hanging out, so he hadn't been back yet.

I grabbed the cat and a cat carrier, and we drove toward Harthaven to meet up with Danny.

"Max looked so sad when we left him," I said as we headed north along the main highway that looped the island.

"It didn't make sense to bring him with us, but I felt bad too," Cody agreed. "We'll take him for a nice long run on the beach when we get back. I want to stop by my place to check in on Mr. Parsons before that, though. When I left him on Friday, Banjo and Summer assured me they planned to stay with him through this morning, but I'm not sure what their plans were for this afternoon and evening."

Banjo and Summer were a hippie couple who lived in a small hut down the beach from Mr. Parsons. They shared a love of old movies and soap opera reruns with him, and often spent time in his mansion, which worked out for Cody and me, because it provided us with some alone time.

"We can stay at your place tonight if that works better. Max is always happy to spend time with Rambler," I said, referring to Mr. Parsons's dog.

"What about Mystic? Do you think he'll be okay in my apartment?"

"I think so. He seems fairly adaptable. I'll just need to let Siobhan know what we're doing if we don't see her later in the day so she can take care of the cats in the sanctuary."

Moving back and forth between the cabin and Cody's place was sometimes inconvenient for one or both of us, but we made it work despite the juggling required.

When we arrived, Danny was waiting for us in the bar parking lot. I wasn't sure why he hadn't gone inside, but he might just have arrived himself. He let us in through the back door, and I set down the cat carrier inside the storage room, figuring that because the murder happened there, starting our search there made sense. I opened the door to the carrier, then stood back and waited for Mystic to do his thing.

I could see the room had already been thoroughly searched from the fact that everything in it had been disturbed. Putting things back the way they'd been was going to be a lot of work for Danny and Aiden. I just hoped word of the murder wouldn't hurt business when they reopened on Tuesday. Though knowing the crowd that hung out at O'Malley's, having a murder to discuss would probably bring in more customers.

Once he was out of the crate, Mystic walked around, as if to get a feel for his environment. He didn't seem intent on any one thing right away, so I gave him his space and began to reshelf some of the items that had been disturbed. As I walked across the room, I noticed an earring slightly under one of the shelves but not so far that it shouldn't have been found by the crime scene guys. I picked it up, then turned toward Danny and Cody. "What do you make of this?"

"It's an earring," Danny answered.

"I know it's an earring, but what do you make of the fact that a woman died in this room on Friday night, which had the crime scene guys spending all of yesterday going through every single item in it, yet I found this earring lying on the floor almost in plain sight."

Danny shrugged. "I guess the crime scene guys who were here might be really bad at their job."

"Or the earring was intentionally left as a test of some sort," I suggested.

"A test?" Danny asked.

"Maybe Mitch left it there to see what you'd do with it. If you're guilty of the murder, you might rush back in here and remove any evidence you found left behind. I bet the crime scene guys came up empty, so they planted the earring."

"I think you've been watching too many cop shows," Danny responded.

I shook my head. "I don't think so. If Mitch only has suspicions and needs proof, it would make sense he'd hope you'd lead him to it."

"What proof?" Danny asked.

"Maybe he hopes you'll go for the murder weapon, or you'll cover up evidence."

"That's nuts," Danny said.

"Is it?" I raised a brow. Okay, I knew I was stretching things a bit, but I didn't trust Mitch Bronson and knew he was up to something.

Danny looked doubtful, which I guess I understood. "So you're suggesting Bronson planted the earring knowing I'd find it and is waiting to see whether I'll notify him or keep the information to myself."

I shrugged. "I guess when you say it out loud it does sound like a lame idea, but I could see Mitch doing something like that to try to tip your hand if he needs something from you he doesn't have. Being able to prove that you suppressed what most people would consider to be evidence might help his case under the right set of circumstances."

"How would he be able to prove I suppressed evidence if I kept quiet?" Danny said. "If he admitted he knew the earring was in here and I found it but didn't report it, he'd have to admit he planted it."

"True," I admitted. "And this isn't even Monica's earring. She had big gold hoops dangling from her ears on Friday night."

"The fact that an earring was on the floor in plain sight does seem strange, but I don't buy Bronson planting it," Cody chimed in. "Still, I think we should be safe and report it."

"Should I call Finn or Bronson?" Danny asked.

"Call Bronson," Cody suggested. "Tell him you just got home and decided to clean up the bar and found the earring."

"I don't know," I countered. "I don't trust Mitch. I'd call Finn. He'll know how to handle it." I glanced around the room for the cat. He seemed to have disappeared while we were talking. "Ask Finn about Monica's shoes while you're at it."

"Monica's shoes?" Danny asked.

"When I found the body on the floor, all I saw was a foot. A bare foot. I don't know if there was a shoe on the other foot, but the one that was sticking out from under the tarp was definitely bare. I'm just curious what happened to that shoe. Did the killer toss it under the tarp? If the shoe was missing, was it ever found? And if not, where is it?"

"I remember the shoes she had on," Danny said. "Several of the guys commented on the unique color."

"A really bright green," I remembered.

"And the heels were high," Danny added. "At least three or four inches. I remember wondering how she could even walk in them. It makes sense that if she was involved in a struggle, she might have kicked them off, but it seems Finn would have found them when he first looked around. I'll call him to ask."

Danny took out his phone. Finn agreed with Cody that it was best he call Mitch directly. He thought it was a good thing Cody and I were with Danny when he came back to the bar for the first time. If Mitch was having the place watched, he'd know Danny hadn't returned before we all arrived together, so any evidence that was found wouldn't be suspect. Of course, Finn admitted that if Mitch really wanted to nail Danny, he'd find a way.

As for the shoes, Finn confirmed that when the tarp was removed, Monica was barefoot. He'd looked around but hadn't found her shoes. Again, I asked, where were they?

I went in search of Mystic while Danny continued his conversation with Finn. I didn't see him in the storage room and we'd left the door open, so he could have wandered out into the hallway. The doors to both bathrooms as well as the office were closed, so I headed down the hallway to the bar. I found him behind the bar itself, swatting at something beneath it that he couldn't quite reach. I got down on my stomach to take a look. It was dark, so I took out my phone and used the flashlight app to help brighten the tight space beneath the bottom of the bar and the floor. It took my eyes a minute to focus, but then I spotted something shiny on the floor. I'd need to slip something under the bar to pull the object toward me, so I got up and went into the kitchen, figuring I could use a long fork or some other long, thin object. I picked a pair of prongs and took them back to the bar. I laid down again and worked whatever it was toward me. Once it was out of the confined space, I picked it up and gasped. Hidden under the bar where Danny, Aiden, and Siobhan had been working on Friday night was a necklace with a gold heart with the letters *DH ♥ MC* stamped on the front.

"Danny Hart loves Monica Caldron," I whispered. I remembered that necklace. Danny had given it to her when they'd dated back in high school. She'd worn it all the time back then. I guess she might have kept it even though she and Danny had broken up more than a decade ago. She might even have been wearing it on the night she was murdered, although I didn't remember seeing it around her neck, and she'd been telling everyone she was on the island to hook up with Cody, which would indicate she wasn't interested in my brother. Still, Danny did say she was all over him when he hauled her into the hallway, and I'd seen her flirting with every other man in the bar. There was no doubt about it in my mind: Monica had her own agenda that didn't always make sense. For all I knew, she was after Cody *and* Danny. It would seem she must have been wearing the necklace at some point on Friday night, though the fact that the necklace had ended up beneath a bar very few people had access to was bringing up a lot of questions I wasn't sure I wanted answered.

I decided the best course of action now was to ask Danny about the necklace. I was about to head back to the storage room to do just that when Mitch Bronson showed up at the front door. I slipped the necklace in my pocket and let him in.

"Ms. Hart," he said.

"Deputy Bronson. I assume you're here in response to Danny's call about the earring."

"I am."

I stepped aside so he could pass. "Cody and Danny are in the back. And just so you know, I'm the one who found the earring, so it'll have my prints on it if you check."

"Good to know."

I led the way to the storage room, where Cody and Danny were still cleaning up. They hadn't been talking, which was probably a good thing, because Mitch would have been able to hear whatever they were saying as he approached.

"It would have been nice if your men had returned things to their proper places when they were done tearing the place apart," Danny commented as Mitch entered the room. "Everything was totally trashed."

"It isn't their job to clean up after themselves. It's their job to uncover physical evidence. I understand you found an earring."

Danny handed it to him. Mitch took it with a gloved hand and put it in an evidence bag.

"Monica wasn't wearing that earring on Friday," I said. "I remember she had on big hoops."

"Noted," Mitch replied.

"And the earring was found in plain sight," Danny added. "I don't see how your men could have missed it."

Mitch frowned. "Has anyone other than you been here since the tape was removed this morning?"

"Not that I know of," Danny answered. "I've been staying at my brother's since Friday night. I came back for the first time with Cait and Cody just a short time ago. The only other person to have a key is my brother, and we've been together the whole weekend."

Mitch held up the evidence bag and looked at the earring inside. "Okay. Well, thank you for calling me so quickly. And let me know if anything else turns up."

With that, he left.

"Well, he was downright pleasant," I said.

Danny frowned. "Yeah. Almost too pleasant."

"The man's a professional doing an important job," Cody reminded us. "I'm sure he's capable of setting aside any personal animosity he has toward Danny to do that job." Cody looked around the room. "The cat didn't seem to find anything in here. Was he interested in anything in the bar?"

"No," I said, although I had no idea why I said that. I could certainly be honest with both Danny and Cody, but for some reason I had the feeling we were being watched, or at least listened to. I was pretty sure someone from the sheriff's office couldn't legally install a listening device without a warrant and I doubted he had enough on Danny to get one, but that didn't mean someone else wasn't listening in.

"Let's finish cleaning up and then head back to the cabin." I looked at Danny. "We can pick up a pizza and discuss things. I'll call the others to see if they want to join us."

Danny sighed. "Sounds good. Suddenly, I'm finding this place pretty depressing."

It took us over an hour to make the storage room functional again. Mystic was using his time to wander around the bar, checking things out. Other than the necklace, which I planned to ask Danny about when we were away from here, the only other thing he paid any attention to was a slip of paper he'd found on the floor with a partial phone number written on it. There'd been a lot of people in the bar on Friday; I was certain at least a few phone numbers were exchanged, so I didn't necessarily feel it was relevant, but the cat had been batting at it. I had to at least consider it might provide a clue. Of course, for it to be of any help at all, we'd need to figure out the last two digits. I supposed there were only a limited number of combinations. If need be, we could try them all, although that was likely to take a whole lot of time that might be better spent on other things.

Cody offered to help Danny carry several cases of liquor from the storage room into the bar. A lot of drinks had been served on Friday, so supplies had been pretty well depleted. Danny offered to call Aiden to help in his stead, but Cody said he was happy to do what was needed, so I decided to try calling Adam Goldberg, the last man on the suspect list Cody and I had, one more time. To this point he hadn't answered the phone or returned any of my messages.

"Yeah," Adam answered after the fourth ring. I didn't know him well, but we were acquainted, and I was put off by his gruff tone.

"Adam," I tried for a cheery tone myself. "Hi. It's Cait Hart. Did you get my messages?"

"I got 'em."

"I see." This conversation wasn't going very well. "So I guess you know I'm talking to people who were at the reopening of O'Malley's on Friday night. I don't know if you've heard, but Monica Caldron was found dead in a back room."

"I heard."

Okay. I didn't understand the defensiveness, unless he actually was the killer, but at least he knew what had happened so I wouldn't need to take a lot of time explaining things. I'd need to keep it casual or he'd probably just hang up on me. "I know you dated Monica a few times since she'd been back on the island. I also understand things ended badly between you. I'm not sure if you spoke to her on Friday, but I understand you saw each other on Thursday evening. I hoped she might have shared something with you that could help us find out what happened on Friday."

"Are you trying to pin her murder on me?" he asked.

I could see I was just making things worse, although I was beginning to suspect he did know something. Otherwise, I didn't feel his tone was warranted. "No. I'm not trying to pin Monica's murder on anyone. I'm just trying to find out what happened."

I could hear a lot of noise in the background. I wasn't sure where Adam was, but I was pretty sure he wasn't alone. Perhaps I should have waited to speak to him in person.

"I know you Hart siblings are a tight group, and I know you all defend one another, but I think you might be barking up the wrong tree if you're trying to help your brother."

"Why do you say that?" I asked, again wishing I'd never called him at all.

Adam answered. "I saw Danny on Friday night. I was coming out of the bathroom when I saw him pull Monica into the hallway. I didn't see what happened before that, but I've since learned you and she had a bit of a brawl."

"I wouldn't call our altercation a brawl. She pushed me down and I called her on it."

"Whatever. What I know is that she was madder than a cat in hot water. When Danny first pulled her into the hallway, they were both yelling. I wasn't sure who was the madder of the two. I stopped to watch, but after Monica started biting him, Danny pulled her into the back room. I didn't stick around after that; I had my own date waiting on me, but from the yelling and cussing I heard coming from that room, there's no doubt in my mind Danny was the one to finally shut her up. I told the visiting deputy as much. If you want to know more about things, I suggest you talk to him."

Chapter 5

After a bit of back and forth between the members of the sleuthing group, we decided we'd meet at Finn and Siobhan's again. It used to be that my cabin was sleuthing central, but now that we had Connor to consider, it made more sense to meet at their house so they could put him to bed when the time came. I missed having the meetings in my space, but it wasn't inconvenient for me to walk across the lawn to the house Aunt Maggie had given to my sister and brother-in-law. I guess the new location was further proof things were changing, and if I didn't want to get left behind, I needed to get on board.

As Cody and I had planned, we took Max for a walk along the beach when we got home. Danny was going to head back to Aiden's for a while, and then the brothers would meet us all for dinner. That gave Cody and me time to check in with Mr. Parsons. Though he could be cranky at times, he was a sweet old guy, and I had a huge soft spot in my heart for him. When we showed up with Max, he and Rambler wanted to play, so we ended up taking both dogs for a fairly long walk along the beach.

"I've been thinking about Mr. Parsons's house," Cody said as we walked along the waterline hand in hand.

"What about it?"

"My apartment on the third floor has been perfect for me, with a spare room for an office. But I'm not sure it's going to be big enough once we marry, and especially not when we start a family. I spoke to Mr. Parsons, who has no plans to use the second floor at all. What would you think about remodeling that space? I'm thinking we can create a big kitchen, dining area, and living area on the third floor, and move the bedrooms down to the second floor. There are five large bedrooms there, which would give us plenty of space for a big master suite, a couple of guest or kids' rooms, and an office we could share."

I paused to consider Cody's suggestion. It seemed like a huge undertaking, but I supposed we could live on the third floor while the second floor was being renovated. Cody's apartment was adequate for the two of us, but he was right about it being tight when we had children. We'd never decided on a number of kids, but I knew we both wanted at least three.

"I like it," I said. "Maybe we can even open up the space a bit on the third floor. I'd love to have the interior walls removed so the entire space was one large area. The view from up there is amazing. It would be nice to add additional windows to the wall facing the ocean."

"I love that idea. I'll have to get an engineer to look at the supports before we start tearing down walls or adding windows, but the concept sounds amazing."

I loved the fact that Cody understood my hesitation in leaving my little cabin and was going out of his way to make me equally excited about the new home we would have, but the old mansion had been in Mr. Parsons's family for four generations, which was something to consider. I picked up a stick and tossed it for the dogs. "Are you sure all this is okay with Mr. Parsons? We're talking about some pretty major renovations and it's his family home."

"I already spoke to him. He wants us to do whatever we want with the house. He intends for us to raise a family there, and he has no children to hand the house and land down to. I think he really values that we've both gone out of our way to make sure he's taken care of, and he wants us to be happy and comfortable."

I leaned my head on Cody's shoulder. "I guess it would be fun to completely remodel everything. I love what you've done with the third floor, but it does have a bachelor pad vibe. It would be nice to lighten things up a bit. I've never decorated a house before. When I moved into Maggie's cabin, it was already perfect, so I just left it as it was. I even used the dishes, bedding, and furniture that were already there."

"Maybe we should draw out our vision and get an architect over to look at things. It will be loud and messy for a while, which could become an issue. We'll need to be sure Mr. Parsons isn't stressed by all the people coming and going. I even considered getting him a room in town while the major renovations are taking place."

"We'll definitely need to be sensitive to Mr. Parsons's health issues. Balthazar has a huge house on the north shore near Alex with only him living in it. They get along really well. Maybe we could work it out for Mr. Parsons to stay there for a week or two during the demolition phase."

Cody paused and kissed me firmly on the lips. "That, my wife-to-be, is a very good idea."

Wife-to-be. I liked the sound of that. I just hoped Cody would be able to deal with his mother as perfectly as he'd dealt with the house issue. I really wanted to get married on Madrona Island, but I didn't want her to hate me before we had a chance to establish what I hoped would be a warm and loving relationship.

By the time we'd taken Rambler back to Mr. Parsons and deposited Max at my cabin, the rest of the gang had shown up at the big house. Danny and Aiden had brought pizza for everyone, and Finn had picked up some beer. It seemed obvious by the energy in the room that we were all determined to figure out what had happened.

"Can I talk to you for a minute?" I asked Danny before I settled in.

"Sure. What's on your mind?"

"Let's go outside."

He looked confused by my request but didn't argue. "What's up?" he asked after we'd stepped out onto the porch.

I held up the broken necklace. "I found this under the bar this afternoon. I was going to ask you about it, but Mitch Bronson showed up just then, so I put it in my pocket." I dangled the necklace from my fingers.

"I recognized it as the one you gave to Monica in high school."

Danny took the necklace from me. "Yeah, it's that necklace. Monica came into the bar last week while I was getting the place stocked for the reopening celebration. She'd been drinking, even though it was only around four o'clock. She said she missed me, missed us. I could see she was looking for a hookup, but I knew she'd been hooking up with every man in town since she'd been on the island, so I told her I wasn't interested. She started to cry, a ploy I've come to recognize as manipulation. I asked her to leave, and she ripped off the necklace and threw it at me. It hit my chest and fell to the floor. I was going to pick it up, but then she used her arm to knock four bottles of vodka to the floor. The good stuff. So I came around the counter, grabbed her arm, and escorted her out the door. I cleaned up the broken glass and the vodka, which was soaking into our newly refinished hardwood floor. To be honest, I forgot about the necklace. It must have gotten kicked under the bar."

"I guess it's a good thing Mitch didn't find it."

"Yeah, a good thing." Danny looked at me. "When you found it, you didn't think that I...?"

I shook my head. "Not even for a minute. There's something else, though. Something I should ask you about before we join the others."

"Okay. What is it?"

"I spoke to Adam Goldberg today. It seems he was just coming out of the men's room when you pulled Monica into the hallway. He saw her bite you, at which point you pulled her into the storage room. He left then, but he heard you arguing."

"Damn it."

"So you did pull Monica in there?"

"Just for a minute. Less than a minute. The woman was a total maniac. She was yelling at me and kissing me and grabbing at things she shouldn't have, all at the same time. What Adam saw was Monica trying to brand me with a hickey. I was trying to reason with her, but she was being totally insane. I pulled her into the storage room so we could speak without being overheard. The next thing I knew, she started to unzip her dress. I knew I needed to get her out of there, so I grabbed her arm again and tossed her out the back door."

"Why didn't you tell Finn about that?"

Danny shrugged. "I don't know. I guess I wasn't thinking clearly that night. Finding Monica dead was a shock. I suppose part of me figured if I admitted to being in the room with her, it would make me look even guiltier. I didn't know anyone was watching, so I suppose I just figured if I didn't bring it up, no one would know."

"You realize the fact that you withheld this information makes you look twice as guilty?"

Danny let out a groan and ran his hand through his thick, dark hair. "Yeah. I messed up big-time. I'll tell Finn now. In fact, I'll come clean with everyone. I wonder if Bronson knows."

"He does. Adam Goldberg told Mitch what he saw."

Danny hung his head. "Great. I'm surprised he hasn't hauled me off to jail yet."

"He probably doesn't have the proof he needs to arrest you, but you can bet he's looking for it."

"Which means we need to find out who really killed Monica before he gets around to it."

"When Monica's body was found, she didn't have her shoes on. I wonder what happened to them."

"I have no idea. Monica was wearing them when I tossed her out the door and told her to go home. Looking back on it, I know I handled things poorly. She was drunk, and if I had to guess, she'd been doing drugs as well. I was angry and worked up, and I realized after I had a chance to think about things that I should have made sure she got home instead of just tossing her into the alley. I didn't kill her, but it's probably my fault she's dead. If I had taken her home, or found someone else to do it, she'd most likely be alive today."

"Maybe," I said. "But until we figure out who killed her, we can't know that for sure."

Danny and I returned to the others. We'd decided to share everything we'd talked about with them. Sure, the fact that Danny had pulled Monica into the storage room and had failed to mention it to anyone made it seem like he'd been intentionally trying to cover it up, but none of us believed he'd killed her, and it seemed best for us to be on the same page.

After we'd all eaten, we settled around the whiteboard. In one way or another, we'd managed to cross everyone off the list of top-tier suspects we'd created the night before. We'd need to take another look at the people who'd been at the bar and come up with a list of individuals we felt were the second most likely suspects. I had the piece of paper with the partial phone number Mystic had found. It seemed an unlikely clue, but I might as well present it to the group.

We spent the next half hour discussing how we might be able to figure out the rest of the number, but eventually, we decided the possibilities were too broad to spend a whole lot of time on it. We turned to tossing around other names from the master list we thought might have a motive to kill Monica. In the end, it was Danny who brought us around to a very cruel reality.

"Monica was back on the island for two weeks," he said. "Based on her behavior, I have to conclude she was either heavily medicated or was experiencing some type of a manic episode. She managed to piss off pretty much everyone she came into contact with. The list of people who were both at the party on Friday and had motive for wanting her out of the way is probably extensive. I suggest we might want to approach this thing from a different angle."

"What angle?" Cassie asked.

"I don't know," Danny admitted, "but unless we're willing to interview every single person who was at the bar when Monica attacked Cait, we most likely won't get where we need to be with the approach we've been taking."

"What we really need is an eyewitness or a piece of physical evidence," Finn said. "It's frustrating not to be part of the investigative team."

I spoke up. "There's the earring I found today. What if it wasn't a plant but something that was left behind by someone who was in the room?"

"It's too bad we don't still have it," Cody said.

"If you can describe it to me, I can probably draw it," Siobhan offered.

Siobhan was an excellent artist, so I spent the next few minutes describing the earring in all the detail I could remember. Then I held up the drawing. "This is pretty good. Does anyone recognize it?"

No one did, but we'd all continue to search our memories.

"I might have something," Tara said. "It's probably nothing, which is why I haven't mentioned it before, but now that we seem to have hit a dead end, I thought I'd bring it up just in case."

"What is it?" Danny asked.

"I stayed behind after Mass today to speak with Sister Mary about the trip the two of us are talking about taking after the first of the year. It was a nice day, so we headed out to Father Kilian's pond and sat down on the little bench he built. We were wrapping up our conversation when I noticed Libby Baldwin talking to Father Bartholomew."

So far, this wasn't a startling occurrence. Libby was a twenty-one-year-old waitress who'd started working at O'Malley's after moving to the island last summer. She was kind of a ditz in a fun, lovable sort of way. I hadn't seen her at St. Patrick's before and didn't think she was a member of the congregation, but I supposed there were a lot of reasons a young woman might seek the confidence of a priest.

"After a moment, I noticed she was crying," Tara continued. "I wondered if she was okay and even considered following her and checking on her after she finished speaking to Father Bartholomew, but then I saw he looked angry. Somehow that didn't sync with the fact that an obviously distressed young woman seemed to be pouring her heart out to him."

"That does sound like an odd meeting," I agreed.

"I said something to Sister Mary," Tara continued. "She turned and looked at them and frowned. She didn't say much, just that she had an idea what was going on and it would be best if I stayed out of it completely."

"Seems like a strange response for her as well," Siobhan said.

"I agree," Tara answered. "And like I said, I have no reason to believe that whatever Libby was talking about had anything to do with Monica or her death, but Libby does work at the bar, she was on the premises when Monica died, and the more I think about it, the more certain I am Libby wore earrings on Friday very similar to the one Cait found. I can't say for certain, though, they were the same."

"I think the earring Cait found is one of the ones the jewelry shop by the wharf in Harthaven sells," Cassie said. "The shop deals in locally made products, and while I can't say for sure the earring Cait found came from there, it looks like the type of thing they carry."

"It sounds like someone needs to have a chat with Libby," Aiden suggested.

"I can check out the jewelry store tomorrow," Cassie offered. "I'll take the drawing Siobhan made and see if the woman who owns the place recognizes it."

"Don't you have class tomorrow?" I asked Cassie.

She looked away. "I'm off this week for midsemester break."

I glanced at Siobhan, who shook her head in a suggestion, I was sure, to let it go.

"I'll talk to Libby," Danny offered. "We get along well and I think she'll talk to me. Should we meet back here again tomorrow?"

"I think we should," I answered. "I have a few ideas to follow up on since the bookstore is closed. Say around five?"

After the meeting started to break up, I pulled Cassie aside. "What's going on with school?" I asked.

"Nothing's going on. I'm just on break."

"Seems like an odd time to have a break," I responded.

Cassie shrugged. "There are midterms this week. I dropped a few of my classes, so I didn't have many to take."

"How many?" I asked.

"How many what?" Cassie asked. I could see by her body language that she was getting ready to shut me out completely. I didn't want that, but I hated to see her quit college before she even got started. On the other hand, I hadn't gone to college at all, and things worked out great for me. College wasn't for everyone; I needed to remember that.

"I was just curious how many midterms you needed to take."

"Just one, and it was from an online course. I finished it before I came home. I would think that instead of hassling me for dropping a few classes you'd be happy to have me home for the week."

I hugged Cassie. "I am happy to have you home. And I didn't mean to hassle you. You're an adult and I know you're perfectly capable of managing your own life. I guess my big-sister instinct just kicked in."

Cassie smiled. "That's okay. There's a lot going on and you're under a lot of stress. Do you and Tara need me to work at the bookstore this week? I could use some cash."

"I'll talk to Tara, but I think we could. Actually, having you there will free me up a bit to work on Monica's murder. You were at the bar that night. Did you notice anything that might provide a clue to what happened to her?"

Cassie shook her head. "I was in the kitchen for most of the night. I couldn't work the bar because I'm not twenty-one, so the only time I left the kitchen was to deliver food and pick up dirty dishes. I do remember seeing Monica and wondering why she was acting so hyper. It was like she was on speed or something. Not that I'm familiar with the various drugs or the behavior associated with them, but she was definitely acting odd."

"Yeah, that seems to be what everyone is saying. Danny mentioned she'd seemed manic ever since she'd been back. I wonder if she didn't actually suffer from bipolar disorder. It would make a lot of what was going on make sense."

"She did seem manic. And overly aggressive. I could almost see where she might have attacked someone she was angry with. I know she died from blunt force trauma to the head. We've been operating under the assumption that someone had a grudge against her and intentionally killed her, but what if someone was just defending themselves? I can see a scenario where someone might have gone down the hallway to use either the ladies' or the men's room. Maybe Monica was pounding on the door to get back in, so this person opened the door, only to have her attack them. They could have struggled and somehow ended up in the storage room. Maybe this person picked something up and hit Monica to get her to back off and the blow hit her just right and she died. I could see how the person who did the hitting might freak out and take off out the back door."

"That's a pretty good theory," I said. "If the killer hit Monica in self-defense, trying to track down individuals with motive to kill her isn't going to get us anywhere. If Monica did die at the hands of someone trying to defend themselves, it could have been anyone."

"I don't know that I'd say *anyone*," Cassie countered. "Most people would have called the police instead of taking off."

I raised a brow. "Would they? I know it seems that anyone of solid moral fiber would have called the cops and reported what happened, keep in mind that Danny, who we both know is a pretty upstanding guy, panicked and didn't tell the entire truth when questioned. I think it's hard to know how you'll respond in a situation until you're actually in it."

"I guess you're right. Whatever happened occurred during a time when almost everyone had been drinking, so judgments were most likely impaired."

"The problem I see if someone did hit Monica in self-defense is that unless they come forward and admit what happened, I don't know how we're ever going to find out about it."

Cassie paused. "Bronson is going to go after Danny as long as he doesn't have another option. He doesn't have a lot, but he might have enough to arrest him."

"Perhaps," I agreed.

"Danny might be in real trouble if we don't figure this out."

I nodded. Mitch wouldn't want to walk away from this until he'd solved it. In a case where he didn't have many suspects, I could totally see him focusing all his energy into digging up evidence, circumstantial or not, to demonstrate that the suspect he did have was guilty.

Chapter 6

Monday, October 29

Cody had some work to do to ensure that the next issue of the *Madrona Island News* was published on time, so he headed into town early on Monday morning. I was off, so I took Max for an early morning run. When we returned to the cabin, I found Mystic sitting on the deck overlooking the water, which was odd because I'd left him inside and I didn't think I'd left any doors or windows open.

"What are you doing out here?" I asked the cat as he jumped down from his perch on a lawn chair to wend his way through my legs.

"Meow."

I bent down with the intention of picking him up, but he scooted away at the last minute. I took a step toward him and he took several more steps away.

"Okay, what's up?" I asked. It seemed apparent the cat had a specific reason to be outside instead of inside, where I'd left him.

"Meow." The cat began to trot down the beach.

I looked at Max, shrugged, and followed. Being led to an unknown destination by one of Tansy's magical cats was an exercise I'd performed many times in the past. After a few minutes, it was apparent Mystic was heading toward Francine Rivers's property. She had two cats, so I hoped this trip wasn't just an excuse for him to visit the feline friends I was sure he could sense. After making our way around the fencing that led out toward the sea, I hiked up onto Francine's lawn to find her watering her flower pots with a hose.

"Cait; Max. How nice to see you," Francine greeted us. She looked at Mystic. "And who is this?"

"This is Mystic," I answered. "He's one of my temporary cats."

"He's absolutely beautiful. Very unique." Francine bent down to pet the cat, who seemed to appreciate her effort.

"I guess you heard about the death we had at O'Malley's the other evening," I said, figuring the cat had led me here for a reason.

Francine stood up. "I did. I spoke to Nora Bradley, who seemed to know quite a bit about the young woman."

"She did?" Nora was the wife of the now-deceased mayor of Madrona Island, a descendent of one of the founding families of the island, and had lived on the island her entire life. She was quite a bit older than Monica, however—at least thirty years older—so I was somewhat surprised to hear the two knew each other.

"Not a lot of people know this, but Monica's biological mother was Riva Cuthwright."

I'd known Monica's mother had died when she was a baby, and her father had remarried. Monica had referred to her stepmother as her mom because the woman had raised her since before she could even remember. Although I'd heard Monica's mom was actually her stepmom, I guess I'd never stopped to consider who had given birth to her. Riva Cuthwright was the daughter of millionaire Dalton Cuthwright, a self-made man who lived on a private island in the area.

"If I remember correctly, Dalton Cuthwright was divorced."

Francine nodded. "Dalton divorced Riva's mother, Gwen Cuthwright, when Riva was young, so she grew up spending part of her time with her mother in Seattle and part of her time with her father on his island. It was during one of her trips to visit her father that she met Monica's father, Tyson Caldron. Tyson and Riva married after a short romance and Monica was born a year later. When Monica was just nine months old, Riva died due to complications from pneumonia. Two years later, Tyson remarried, and his new wife, Janet, is the one who raised Monica."

"Okay, I'm following so far." I frowned. "Dalton Cuthwright recently passed away, didn't he?"

"He did," Francine confirmed. "Nora told me that until six months ago Monica was included in his will. In fact, Nora seemed to think her share of the Cuthwright estate was equal to that of her three Cuthwright cousins."

"You said until six months ago. What happened then?"

Francine wandered over to turn off her hose before she continued. "Keep in mind, everything I'm telling you I heard from Nora, so I have no way of knowing if it's absolute fact. According to Nora, Cuthwright cut Monica out of his will when he learned of her bizarre behavior from one of his grandsons."

Okay, knowing what I knew about Monica's behavior, it made sense.

"Did Monica come to the island to protest the will or to ask for her share?" I wondered. If she had, that would explain why she'd really shown up after all these years.

"Monica contested the will when she found out she'd been cut out. She argued that her cousins had used their influence to rob her of what was rightfully hers when Cuthwright became ill. She further argued that Cuthwright wasn't of sound mind when he altered the document. On the surface, it seemed she might have a legitimate claim, but because of her behavior when she arrived on the island, Nora doubted she would have come out the victor. Still, the cousins had been sweating things since Monica got here. Nora seemed to think she had something on one or all of them. Something bad that could very well influence the outcome of the lawsuit. Of course, now that she's dead, I imagine the whole thing will be dropped."

I narrowed my gaze. "That worked out quite conveniently for the cousins." I knew two of the cousins lived and worked elsewhere, but one of them, Colin Cuthwright, lived with his grandfather on his private island until Dalton died. As far as I knew, Colin was still living there. Furthermore, he spent a lot of time on Madrona Island, and I remembered seeing him at the bar on Friday night. This warranted some further research at the very least.

******

Danny stopped by my cabin later that morning. He wanted to let me know he'd spoken to Libby, who had revealed the subject matter of her conversation with Father Bartholomew.

"Apparently, Father Bartholomew is Libby's uncle," Danny started off.

"Uncle? Really?"

Danny nodded. "Libby told me the reason she moved to Madrona Island in the first place was because her uncle made it sound like a magical place to live."

That much was true. Madrona Island *was* a magical place. I supposed I shouldn't be surprised that Father Bartholomew had a young niece. Even though he was a priest, he'd come from an actual family with parents and siblings.

"So the conversation the pair were having was personal," I said.

Danny nodded. "Libby's pregnant and she's considering having an abortion. Father Bartholomew is obviously against the idea and, according to Libby, he's become quite worked up about it. She's an adult who can do what she wants, but Libby admitted her uncle's passion for her unborn child has her pausing to reconsider things."

Okay, so that would explain the conversation Tara had witnessed, as well as Sister Mary's suggestion not to get involved. "Did you ask Libby about the earring?" I asked.

"I did. She said she has earrings very similar to the one we found, and she bought them from the little boutique Cassie mentioned. But her pair are slightly different and she still has them."

Well, that told us something. Cassie had planned to follow up at the boutique today. Maybe the shop owner would remember who'd purchased this particular pair.

Because it was Danny's butt on the line, I decided to share the information Francine had provided that morning. He knew Colin Cuthwright and remembered seeing him at the bar on Friday. I decided telling Finn what we'd learned now rather than waiting for that evening was a good idea, so I called his cell and asked him to meet me at the newspaper, which was right next door to his office—which, I assumed, would also be occupied by Mitch Bronson.

******

Deputy Bronson hadn't arrived on Madrona Island yet today, so Finn was alone in his office, but we decided to meet in the newspaper office anyway. Cody had taken the initiative to look up the lawsuit Monica had filed after her grandfather passed away and realized she had been cut out of his will. Dalton Cuthwright hadn't offered any explanation for it nor was he required to do so, but when Monica initially complained to her cousins about their manipulating the situation, they'd informed her their grandfather was concerned about Monica's erratic behavior and didn't feel she would be able to handle an inheritance in the manner he expected of her.

It was Cody's opinion, based on what he could find out, that Monica hadn't had much of a case. She'd tried to argue that Cuthwright hadn't been of sound mind when he made the change, but his attorney had stated that his client had been in full command of his mental faculties. Cody found a statement by the judge who initially reviewed Monica's complaint saying it was his opinion that the will had been legally executed and should stand as written.

"So Monica has spent her entire life thinking she's going to receive a pot of money when her grandfather dies, only to find out she'd been cut out of his will," I summarized. "She tries to contest the will using legal channels, but that isn't getting her anywhere, so she comes to the island. To do what?" I asked. "Francine mentioned Nora had told her Monica had been spreading it around that she had some sort of dirt on one or more of her cousins. If we assume she came here to use the dirt she claimed to have as leverage to get some of her grandfather's money, what was up with the crazy behavior?"

"Something isn't fitting," Finn agreed.

"Danny seemed to think Monica was going through some sort of manic episode. If that was true, she might not have had a lot of control over her odd behavior," I said.

"Say that's true," Cody said. "Say her behavior was driven by a mental illness. That still doesn't explain who killed her."

"At this point my money's on Colin Cuthwright," I said. "If Monica did have dirt on one of her cousins, it was probably him."

"Probably," Cody said. "I did some checking. It seems the older two grandsons have good jobs and have amassed their own wealth. Colin, on the other hand, has pretty much sponged off his grandfather his entire life. As far as we know, he was also the only grandson who was on the island at the time of Monica's death. If the motive for her murder was a secret she believed she had, chances are Colin's her killer."

"How do we prove it?" I asked.

"I guess I could have a chat with Colin, although Bronson might consider that to be interference on my part."

"Danny knows him," I said. "It might be best if he's the one to speak to him. I doubt he'll admit it if he did kill Monica, but Danny might be able to at least get a sense of how he felt about her."

"I didn't notice Monica had a purse or phone or anything when her body was found." I looked at Finn.

He frowned. "You're correct. I don't believe a purse or a phone was retrieved at the scene of the murder. As far as I know, Mitch hasn't turned them up either, although I'm sure by now he's searched her motel room."

"Monica was using the room as a decoy," Cody said.

I raised a brow. "Decoy?"

Cody let out a breath. "She came by the newspaper a couple of times. She made it clear she was interested in a hookup, and that while she was checked into a room, she'd also rented a small house on the north shore where she could entertain her friends without everyone in town being up in her business." Cody went over to his desk. He took out a small piece of paper. "She gave me the address." Cody looked at me. "And no, I never went to the house. I never went anywhere with her. It might be worth checking out."

"I agree," Finn said.

"We'll go," I offered. "You need to be careful not to do anything Mitch can use against you with the sheriff."

"Okay. I'll go back to work and focus on the other cases on my desk. We can discuss what you find this evening."

After Finn went back to his office, Cody and I locked up the newspaper office and headed north. I was hurt he hadn't told me about Monica's visits, but I guess he realized her behavior would just upset me, and he most likely wanted to avoid that as much as possible. I knew Cody loved me and I could trust him, but having someone like Monica openly trying to seduce him away from me had gotten under my skin more than I wanted to admit. If it turned out Monica's death hadn't been related to her battle with her cousins, I'd be willing to bet the person who killed her was someone like me, who was just trying to defend their territory.

"I'm sorry I didn't tell you about Monica's visits to the newspaper," Cody said after we'd been traveling in silence for a while. "I knew you'd be upset and I didn't want to upset you for no reason."

"I know," I said. "I'm not mad. I would have been upset and I understand why you chose not to mention it. Monica had a way of getting under my skin like no one else I've ever known."

"She was beautiful and assertive and totally crazy. Not a good combination."

"Yeah. She really had something going on. Initially, I thought she was on the island for the express purpose of seducing you away from me, but the more I hear about her behavior, the more it seems she was intent on seducing half the male population. Danny said she was all over him that night, and had been for more than a week before she died."

Cody turned onto the coast road and headed north. "Given the fact that she had made so many people mad, I think it's going to be hard to narrow things down to a single suspect unless we can find physical evidence."

"I've had the same thought. I never really liked her in high school. I thought she was manipulative and a user, but I don't remember her being crazy or acting so erratically. I wonder what happened to her."

"She might have developed a mental illness as an adult, or she might have gotten hooked on some really bad drugs. The medical examiner must have conducted a toxicology screen. I wonder what he found."

"Is there a way to find out?"

Cody shrugged. "I know someone who works at the lab who might be willing to share information. It's not a sure thing, but Sandra has helped me out when I've been doing research for a news article."

"Sandra Riverton?"

"Yeah. You know her?"

"Not really. She used to live on the island. She wasn't here long, maybe a year or two. She moved after she got the job at the crime lab. I didn't realize the two of you had met."

"She's friends with one of the guys on my softball team. He introduced us a couple of years ago when I was looking for information for an article I was writing. I won't say we know each other well, but she helps me out from time to time. Do we go right or left at the top of the road?"

I looked at the map I'd pulled up on my phone. "Left. If the address she gave you is correct, it looks like we take the fork to the left and then go all the way down to the end of the road."

The house Monica had been staying in was small, but it was set right on the edge of the beach. Cody parked in the empty drive and then we both got out. We walked across the dirt drive to the front door and knocked. As predicated, no one answered. We waited for a minute and then knocked again just to be certain there wasn't a homeowner who was napping.

"Should we break in?" I asked.

Cody looked around. "I guess that's our only option. I just hope Monica really was staying here and we aren't breaking into someone's home."

I frowned and then cupped my hands and peered in through the front window. I didn't see any evidence that someone was home, but I couldn't see any that Monica had been there either. "Monica wanted you to take her up on her offer. Why would she give you a fake address?"

"I guess she wouldn't," Cody said. He tried the knob. "The door's locked. Let's look for an open window."

"If I was staying here, I'd have the windows in the back of the house open so I could hear the waves. Let's start there," I suggested.

We walked around the house to the back. It was set on a beautiful piece of property, and fortunately, we did find an open window. Cody removed the screen and climbed into what appeared to be a room that was used as an office. Then he came around to the front of the house and opened the door for me. The house was quaint and charming but fairly isolated. It was the very last house on the end of a road that serviced only a few other homes.

"I wonder why Monica rented this house," I said when we were both inside. "She was very overt in her flirting and made no secret of her interest in the men she pursued. I don't understand why she'd feel the need for a secret hideaway."

"Yeah, that doesn't seem her style," Cody agreed.

"And to have a room in town as well, where she did seem to be spending time? The whole thing doesn't make sense."

Cody paused. "The way Monica was acting, I can't see why she didn't just invite the men she was after to her motel room."

I stopped to look around. "Do you see anything that definitely belonged to her? I'm going to feel really bad if she wasn't staying here after all, and we're prowling around in someone else's house."

Cody walked into the bedroom. He opened the closet and pulled out a tiny red dress. "Monica was wearing this when she came to see me the first time. And this polka dot blouse looks familiar as well."

"Okay, so I guess we're back to why. Why would she rent this place in addition to the motel room in town?"

Cody began opening drawers. He sifted through each before moving on to the next.

"What are you looking for?" I asked.

"I'm not sure. I guess something that will help us make sense of things. You were spot-on when you said a secret hideaway all the way out here makes no sense. Monica definitely seemed the sort to seek out the spotlight. The motel room in town fits her personality. This place doesn't."

I opened a drawer and pulled out a large envelope. Inside were photos of at least eight different men, all people I knew, all married or in serious relationships. I cringed when I realized they were mostly or completely naked, entangled with Monica in compromising positions. The photos had been taken in this bedroom. "I think I know what Monica was using this house for." I handed Cody the photos.

"She must have been luring involved men out here and then snapping the photos without them knowing what she was doing."

"She must have been blackmailing them," I tossed out the thought I was sure we both shared. "I guess I can see why a house all the way out here on the far end of the island would be a good place to conduct her business. The men probably felt meeting her in this house provided less of a risk to them. They would have realized that hooking up with her in town would increase the risk of them being seen by someone who might rat them out."

"It looks like we have an envelope full of new suspects," Cody said.

I thought about the men whose photos I had just seen. They were good men, most with families. I hated to think any of them would be capable of murder, but in terms of a motive, protecting what you held dear was probably the best one of them all.

Chapter 7

I didn't want to spend any more time looking at the photos than I already had, so Cody went through them and made a list of all the men. I had to admit my faith in the goodness of mankind in general slipped just a bit when I saw some of the names. Three of the men were active members of St. Patrick's. They had wives and children who loved and depended on them. Yes, Monica had been extremely beautiful, and yes, she did have a way about her that drove some men crazy, but the ones in the photos had to have made a conscious decision to make the trip to the north shore, so none could claim that things had happened before they even knew it. As I considered the names on the list, my sense of certainty that we'd find the killer among them intensified.

"It's a really nice day and I'd love to have a BBQ at the cabin," I said. "I know it makes sense to have the meetings at Finn and Siobhan's so they can put

Connor to bed, but it may be the last I can host in the cabin."

"Why do you say that?" Cody inquired.

"There's a storm coming in, and chances are the temperatures will drop as winter approaches. I figure by next summer I'll have moved into Mr. Parsons's house with you and someone else will be living in the cabin."

"And that makes you sad?"

"A little," I admitted. "But that doesn't mean I'm not also excited about our plans. I'll call everyone and let them know I want to host dinner tonight. If Finn and Siobhan want to put Connor down, we can go over to their place after we eat. We'll need to stop by the grocery store because my refrigerator is pretty bare, but we can do that on our way home. I'd love to do steaks, and maybe some crab."

"Sounds good to me. We can get greens for a salad, some crusty French bread from the bakery, and maybe some asparagus to grill. It'll be a perfect last outdoor cookout, if it does end up being the last one we host at the cabin." Cody pulled me into his arms. "I'm sorry this is so hard for you."

"I guess change in general can be difficult at times. Even when the change is something you really want."

Cody kissed the top of my head. "I know what you mean. When I made the decision to leave the SEALs, I felt really torn, even though I knew it was the right decision for me at that time in my life. And I haven't regretted it for a single day since then, but I do understand how change can be difficult. Have you given any thought to what you're going to do with the cabin when you move out?"

"Technically, that would be up to Finn and Siobhan because they own the estate now, but I thought I'd offer it to Cassie. If she sticks with college, which as this point I kind of doubt, she'd have her own place when she comes to visit, and if she moves back to the island, which seems likely, it will be a perfect first home for her, the way it was a perfect first home for me."

"Has Cassie talked to you about dropping out of college?" Cody asked.

"No. Not in so many words. But she did say she dropped some of her classes, and this is midterm week and she's here and not in Seattle. If I had to guess, I'd say she's biding her time until she feels ready to admit it isn't working out for her. I wish she'd get her degree, but I understand her desire to be here too. I felt the same way after high school, and things have worked out just fine for me, so I have no reason to believe they won't for Cassie."

"I'm glad you're keeping an open mind. It'll make it easier for her to do whatever she decides on. So, what are you thinking of for dessert?"

By the time Cody finished up at the newspaper and we stopped by the market and the bakery, it was almost time to start the grill. The gang agreed it was the perfect night for what might be our last cookout of the season. I didn't mention that this might be my last time hosting a cookout at the cabin because I needed to talk to Finn and Siobhan about things, but the fact that this might be my last hurrah was very much on my mind as the others began to gather. "Wow, steak and crab," Aiden said. "What's the occasion?"

"It just felt like this might be our last chance to grill for the season and I wanted to make it nice," I answered.

"It really is a gorgeous evening," Tara commented as she sipped her wine.

"Enjoy it while you can. I hear there's a storm blowing in tomorrow evening," Cassie informed us.

"I hope it blows through before Wednesday," Danny said. "We're planning a big Halloween celebration at the bar."

"Did Bronson clear you to reopen?" Tara asked.

Danny nodded. "We're good to go. We're opening on schedule tomorrow. It will feel odd after everything that's happened. I'd hoped the murder case would be resolved by now, but I suppose it isn't unusual for these things to take time. Still, I feel like we're getting low on strong leads."

Cody and I hadn't mentioned the pictures we'd found to the group yet. I wanted to eat first, so I just commented that we'd uncovered some information but wanted to wait to discuss the case until after we enjoyed the meal Cody and I had prepared. Cassie brought up the Halloween festivities that were taking place around town, and conversation moved to the usually highly anticipated holiday taking place in just two days' time. Somehow, with everything that had been going on, I'd almost missed what was usually one of my favorite days of the year.

Once dinner was over, the others helped us clean up and then we all trooped over to Finn and Siobhan's so Connor could be put to bed. First, Cassie told us that she'd gone to the boutique where she suspected the earring I'd found in the storage room had been purchased, and confirmed with the owner that the earring was one of hers, but she didn't have a record of who bought that pair. Siobhan shared that she'd spoken to one of her friends, a nurse who'd been in the bar on Friday night, who'd noticed that Monica's eyes were dilated, seeming to indicate she'd probably been on something stronger than alcohol.

Before Cody and I had the chance to bring up the photos, Finn shared that, after he'd completed a series of interviews, Mitch Bronson had come to the conclusion that Danny hadn't killed Monica. Initially, witness statements, along with his proximity to the victim, had made him look guilty, but Mitch had tracked down three different individuals who'd heard Monica arguing with someone after Danny had returned to the bar.

"That's great," I said. I looked at Danny. "You must be so relieved."

"I am. Finn called me earlier, but I thought I'd wait to deliver the news until after we'd had our delicious meal. I knew once the conversation got started, it would be difficult to rein it in."

"Do we know who she was arguing with?" I asked.

"We don't," Finn answered. "Bronson said two women who'd gone to the ladies' room after Danny had returned to the bar both swore they heard Monica's voice coming from inside the storage room. Neither was able to identify who Monica was arguing with, but both agreed the voice was male."

"And the male witness?" I asked.

"He agreed with the two women that he'd heard Monica's voice coming from inside the storage room but didn't know who she was arguing with either. He made a couple of guesses Bronson was following up on. The good news is, the sheriff has put me back on the case. Bronson is going to provide me with an update in the morning and then he plans to go back to San Juan Island to let me finish the investigation."

"That is good news," I said, feeling more than just a little relieved. "Cody and I have news as well, only ours is a lot more disturbing and a lot less positive."

Between us, we filled the group in on our trip to the north shore. Like me, the others were very disappointed to hear that men we knew and considered friends had been pulled into Monica's web of seduction. It was even harder to deal with the idea that one of the men on the list was more than likely the killer.

Once the list had been presented, we all pitched in to narrow it down. We quickly agreed that three of the eight men hadn't been at the bar on Friday night and so most likely wasn't the killer. Additionally, two others, Frank Overland and Len Bingham, had been there with their wives. While it was possible one or the other could have snuck away to kill Monica, Danny's recollection was that both couples had left before my altercation with Monica took place, which was what had set events in motion. Aiden, Tara, and I were also sure the couples had left earlier in the evening.

That just left three men. All had been at the bar, and all had come either alone or with male friends.

"So what now?" Cassie asked. "Are we just going to go up to these guys and tell them we suspect Monica may have been blackmailing them and, as a result, they're on our short list of murder suspects?"

"I don't think that approach would be very effective," I replied.

"Ed Trauner, Gil Varner, and Jeff Golden are all married men with children," I began. "They're all respected members of the community, and I'm sure they'd be highly motivated to ensure that Monica's photos didn't get out. Having said that, I don't see any of them as killers."

"Someone murdered her," Tara pointed out.

Yes, someone had killed Monica. I just hoped it wasn't any of the men on the list. "Let's not forget Colin Cuthwright," I said. "If Monica had dirt on him that might affect his inheritance, it would make him a prime suspect in my book. Besides, out of everyone on the list, he seems the most likely to kill someone who got in the way of what he wanted or needed."

"I agree," Siobhan said. "Let's be sure he stays on the list until we can clear him."

"Okay," Finn said. "That leaves us with Ed Trauner, Gil Varner, Jeff Golden, and Colin Cuthwright. Now that I'm back on the case, I think I should be the one to speak to all four of them. I'll do that tomorrow and we'll see where we end up."

After that, we shared the dessert Cody and I had picked up at the bakery and then parted for the evening. I thought Cody might want to stay at Mr. Parsons's tonight, but he'd checked with him earlier and so felt comfortable staying at the cabin if I wanted to. I found I did want to; very much, in fact. Now that my days at the cabin were numbered, I felt the need to spend as much time there as I could.

Back at the cabin, Cody lit a fire in the outdoor pit while I poured some wine. We cuddled up on the back-porch swing and looked out at the waves that were rolling gently onto the shore. It was calm and peaceful, beautiful and serene. In a word, perfect.

"I spoke to my mother," Cody said after a few minutes of swinging in silence.

I turned to look at him. "And…?"

"And I think I've come up with a compromise that will make everyone happy. Or at least mostly happy. I don't suppose anyone is getting everything they might want, but it's a compromise that will allow us to get married on Madrona Island with my mother's blessing."

From the hesitant tone in Cody's voice, I hated to even ask, but I did. "So what's the compromise?"

"My mom will agree to our getting married on Madrona Island. She'll attend the ceremony with a smile on her face and won't bring up the fact that my grandfather won't be able to be there. I've convinced her that Grandpa will be just as happy to attend remotely because even if the ceremony were in Florida, he'd have a hard time sitting through the entire Mass. We've agreed that allowing him to be part of the wedding via Skype is a workable option."

"Okay. So far, that sounds like a wonderful plan, but I sense a *however* in the mix."

Cody nodded. "However, my mother insists that because the wedding won't be in Florida, we spend the two weeks from Christmas to New Year's there."

"Christmas? But that's the busiest time of the year at the bookstore."

"I know that, and I even made that point, but my mother's adamant that if we're getting married on Madrona Island, we should spend our first Christmas as a married couple with her. I know it'll be tough for you to be gone, but Tara has Willow and Cassie now. I'm sure she could hire part-time help as well. I want you to have everything you want, and if you're serious about not wanting to start our married life with my mother angry at us, I think this is the best compromise."

I wanted to scream that there was no way I wanted to spend Christmas away from my family, but I held my tongue. I knew Cody had worked hard to come up with a plan that would make both me and his mother happy. I hated that he was in the middle of things. A wedding should be a happy event and so far, all it had been was stressful.

"What about Mr. Parsons's Christmas Eve party?"

Cody and I had hosted a party at Mr. Parsons's house for the past three years and I knew he really looked forward to it.

"I thought of that. And I know he'll be disappointed. But I thought maybe we could do a huge Thanksgiving feast at his house instead. We could invite all our friends and family, plus everyone we would have invited to the Christmas Eve party. We could set up tables in the ballroom and serve turkey with all the fixings. We could make it really nice."

I had to admit that sounded reasonable. Mr. Parsons would be disappointed, but he would enjoy the Thanksgiving celebration, and I knew he wanted Cody to be happy and to work out the issues we were having with the wedding.

"I'll make sure Summer and Banjo can stay with him while we're gone so he won't be alone," Cody added. "And Francine will be sure he has a very nice Christmas."

"Okay," I said.

"Okay?" Cody asked.

"Okay. Let's get married."

Cody pulled me into his arms. I could tell he was relieved. I was sure the poor guy had been sweating this talk since the moment he spoke to his mother.

"When should we do it?" I asked.

"I know it's quick, but I think it would be best if we were already married before we went to Florida so my mom can't try to manipulate the situation once we get there."

"Okay," I said again. "How about next month?"

"That works for me," Cody said. "But that isn't a lot of time for you to get ready."

"I don't want a fancy wedding. In fact, I want something really simple. Just family and close friends. We'll have the ceremony in the church and the reception here at Finn and Siobhan's."

Cody smiled. "It sounds perfect."

I pulled out my phone and looked at the calendar. "It'll get really busy at the store after Thanksgiving, so how about Saturday, November 17?"

"The seventeenth sounds perfect. I guess we should check with Father Bartholomew to make sure the church is free."

"I'll call him tomorrow." I settled back and looked out at the sea. I felt a little nervous about everything we'd just discussed. I mean, I'd agreed to getting married in less than three weeks. Holy cow, what had I just gotten myself in to?

Chapter 8

Tuesday, October 30

Coffee Cat Books was busy the next morning, so Tara and I hadn't had the opportunity to chat. Cassie had come in to help out for the week, and Willow had agreed to work half days as well. I was curious to find out what, if anything, Finn might be able to uncover now that he was back on the murder case, but truth be told, what was really occupying my mind, was my upcoming nuptials. Cody had called Father Bartholomew, who confirmed the church was available on the seventeenth, although he was concerned we wouldn't have time to go through the counseling program required of each couple before they were married in the Catholic Church. Cody explained the reason for our haste, and eventually, Father Bartholomew agreed to make an exception and allow us to marry without having completed all the sessions.

I knew Cody was going to ask Danny to be his best man; they had been best friends for years. I'd been Siobhan's maid of honor and considered asking her to stand up for me, but Tara was my best friend, so I was asking her. I'd ask Siobhan and Cassie to be bridesmaids and Cody would ask Aiden and Finn to serve as groomsmen. I'd already decided everyone could just wear something they already owned given the tight timeline. I knew Aunt Maggie would make me a dress that was both simple and beautiful and planned to call her later in the day.

"Can I talk to you for a minute?" I asked Tara once the crowd from the first ferry had dispersed.

"Sure. What's up?"

"Let's go into the office."

Tara followed me with a look of concern on her face. "Is everything okay?"

"Everything's great, but Cody and I have come to a decision and it affects you."

Tara looked cautious. "Okay."

"You know I've been stressing over the situation with Cody's mother and her insistence that we marry in Florida."

"Yes. I'm aware of the situation and the grief it's caused."

"Cody worked out a compromise that will allow us to get married on Madrona Island, but in exchange we have to agree to spend two weeks in Florida over Christmas and New Year's."

Tara smiled. "You're finally going to set a date?"

"We are. I mean, we have. I wanted to talk to you right away because that's our busiest time."

Tara hugged me. "Oh my God, Cait. You're getting married. I'm so happy for you. Don't worry about the bookstore. We'll figure it out. So when's the wedding?"

"November 17."

"This November 17?"

I nodded. "We didn't want to wait. I know it's less than three weeks away, but I really want a small, simple wedding with family and close friends."

Tara hugged me again. "I'm so happy for you. I can't believe my best friend is getting hitched."

"I can't believe it either. Will you be my maid of honor?"

Tara started to cry. She managed to nod her head before she wrapped me in a hug so tight, I wasn't sure I could breathe. I asked her not to say anything to anyone until I had the chance to tell my mother. After Mom, I'd tell Siobhan and Cassie, and then I'd call Maggie to fill her in. I'd done a rough count in my head and I figured I had about twenty-five calls to make. We didn't have time to send out formal invitations; a telephone invite would have to do.

******

"Maggie is thrilled about making my dress," I told Cody over lunch. "She's coming to the island tomorrow to take my measurements. I need to choose the style and fabric. I'm thinking simple, but Siobhan has a bunch of bride magazines left from when she got married, so I'm going over to her place this evening so we can go through them to narrow in on a design."

Cody seemed to be all grins today, which was making me happy. "I thought I'd just wear my black suit, if that's okay with you."

"That sounds perfect."

"Danny, Aiden, and Finn all have black suits too, so we already have the male side of the wedding party taken care of."

"I told Tara, Cassie, and Siobhan to wear whatever they wanted, but Siobhan seemed to think they could find a way to coordinate without going to too much trouble. Cassie and Siobhan are going to take care of all the food, including the cake, and my mom is ordering and paying for the flowers; she just wants me to give her a list of preferred colors. I told her to keep it simple, but she asked me to stop off at the florist to look at options. We'll need to pull together a guest list so I can give Siobhan a head count for the reception, which we plan to have at her house."

"We both want to keep it small, so we should be able to come up with a list pretty quickly. I'll need to make reservations at the inn for my family. I think they'll just need three rooms. It's the off-season, so I'm hoping the short notice won't be a problem."

I took a sip of my water. "I'm sure they have the rooms, but it would be best to check right away. I can't believe we're getting married so soon."

"Are you sure this is what you want?"

I leaned forward and kissed Cody on the lips. "Absolutely."

"That's good, because it feels just right to me too. Oh, I spoke to Mr. Parsons. He totally understands about the Christmas Eve party and loves the idea of a Thanksgiving celebration. Of course, that's going to mean we have to plan a wedding and then follow that up with a meal for about fifty people less than a week later. Is that going to be too much?"

I shook my head. "It'll be fine, and I want to do this for Mr. Parsons. Tara and I talked about it. The store is really slow before Thanksgiving. It's crazy busy beginning with Black Friday, but the week before is really slow, so I'm going to take the week before the wedding off and the week after, right up to Black Friday. That will give me time for last-minute wedding preparations, the two of us a couple of days of alone time, and several days to shop and prepare for the Thanksgiving feast. I went ahead and let my family know about Thanksgiving when I called them about the wedding, and everyone is on board for the change in venue this year. Now all we have to do is hope and pray Monica's murder is solved before then so we don't have it hanging over our heads."

"The pressure to solve it isn't quite as intense now that Danny seems to be off the hook," Cody pointed out.

"Maybe, but I want to see this through."

"Yeah," Cody agreed. "Me too."

"I feel like we've uncovered a lot of suspects. In fact, of all the cases we've worked on, I think this one has the largest number of suspects. The problem is, none of them has panned out. I think the blackmail angle is a strong one. Maybe Finn will turn something up today."

"I guess we're down to just the four suspects we talked about last night. Unless Monica was blackmailing men whose photos weren't in the envelope. I think Finn needs to take a look at her banking records. You'd think there should be a paper trail of some sort."

"Maybe, but I can also see her handling everything with cash. Still, if she was collecting cash from these men, where is it?"

"Good question." Cody looked at his watch. "I need to go. If you're getting together with Siobhan this evening, I think I'll spend some time with Mr. Parsons. Maybe I'll take him out to dinner. I'll come over to the cabin afterward."

"Okay." I scooted out of the booth. "Sounds like a plan. If you talk to Finn and he has news, call me."

"I will." Cody leaned forward and kissed me. "I'll see you this evening."

******

At the bookstore after lunch, Tara and I gave the cat lounge a good cleaning while Cassie and Willow held down the fort in the front.

"So, are visions of wedding dresses dancing around in your head?" Tara asked as she filled a bucket to handle the windows.

"Actually, my head is filled with visions of murder suspects."

Tara paused and looked at me. "Really? You're getting married in less than three weeks and you're still focused on Monica's murder? I figured now that Danny has been cleared and Finn is back on the case, you'd drop it."

"You would think. But no. I feel like I need to finish what I started."

Tara began to squeegee the windows. "Have you talked to Finn today? He was going to talk to the three suspected blackmail victims still on the list. Maybe he's already solved the case and you just aren't aware of it yet."

"Maybe," I acknowledged. "I plan to call him in a bit, but there's something bothering me."

Tara paused and looked at me. "Okay. What's bothering you?"

"In every other murder investigation I've been involved in, the cat Tansy sends has been instrumental in tracking down the killer. Some cats are more active in the investigation than others, and Mystic has been the least active ever, but for some reason I still feel he's with me on it."

"Okay. So what information has he provided so far?" Tara asked.

"He sent me two places: the bar and Francine's. When we went to the bar, I found the earring in the storage room, which still hasn't been identified, a necklace that belonged to Monica and Danny admitted she threw at him, and the phone number with the two last digits torn from the page. Francine told me about Monica's lawsuit with her cousins over their grandfather's inheritance."

Tara used a brush to scrub the next window. "Let's start with the bar. The phone number seems kind of random, but if the cat led you to the earring, maybe that's the clue you need to focus on."

"No." I shook my head. "The cat didn't actually lead me to the earring. I found it myself. The cat didn't pay a bit of attention to it."

"Walk me through what happened."

I began wiping down the leather furniture. "When we arrived at the bar, Danny was waiting for us in the parking lot. We went inside and directly into the storage room. The cat was in a carrier, which I brought inside. I let him out in the room."

"And what *did* he pay attention to?"

"Nothing, really. He just sort of looked around, and then I spotted the earring on the floor. I picked it up, and Danny, Cody, and I began to discuss what it might mean. By the time we'd come up with a plan to deal with the earring, the cat had taken off. I'd left the back-room door open when we went in, so I went out to the bar to look for him. I found Mystic batting at something under the bar. I got down on my stomach to see what it was and found the necklace Danny had given Monica in high school. I asked him about it, and he admitted she'd been by a few days before, when he was in the bar alone. She came on to him and he turned her down. She ripped off the necklace, which she'd been wearing, and threw it at him. It bounced off his chest and fell to the floor. He figured it must have gotten kicked under the bar."

Tara began to squeegee the window she'd just washed. "And what happened next?"

"Mitch Bronson came in through the front door. Danny had called him about finding the earring. I went with Mitch into the storage room, where Danny and Cody were cleaning up."

"And the cat?" Tara asked.

"I lost track of him when Mitch came in. After he left, I went to look for the cat again. I found him batting at something under one of the booths. That was the piece of paper with the partial phone number. I suppose it could be the clue the cat brought me to the bar to find, but it would be pretty weird if the killer's phone number just happened to be on a piece of paper I happened to find on the floor."

"The earring makes a better clue," Tara said.

I frowned. "Except that the cat really wasn't interested in the earring. And three different people said they heard Monica arguing with someone who sounded like a guy after Danny tossed her out. I'm curious who the earring belongs to, but my intuition tells me it isn't the reason the cat wanted me to go to the bar."

"So the phone number?" Tara used a rag to wipe the edges of the windows.

"Maybe. We thought there were too many possible outcomes when we tried to plug in the last two numbers, but if one of the people we already identified is the killer, all we'd need to do is to get their phone numbers to see if any of them have one that matches the digits we have."

Tara pushed the bucket of water off to the side. "That's a great idea. A lot of the people we've eliminated have been cut only because they seemed surprised to hear Monica was dead or we didn't think they could be guilty. I'd take a second look at everyone who's ever been on the list."

"Right. I'll call Cody and have him pull phone numbers. Who knows, maybe we'll find a match."

Two hours later, Cody called to say none of the suspects on our list had phone numbers with the first five digits on the partial we had. I also spoke to Finn, who'd spoken to the three men in Monica's photographs. None admitted to killing her, although none had alibis solid enough to remove them from the list either. Tara suggested maybe the cat was batting at something else under the booth, not the phone number. It was true the paper was on the floor right there in the front of the booth and I hadn't looked further. I called Danny to tell him I wanted to take a second look in the bar. He asked me to come before it opened at four. Tara had adequate help today, so I said I'd be over within the next fifteen minutes.

"It was this booth here," I said to Danny after he'd congratulated me on finally setting a wedding date.

Danny pulled the booth away from the wall. Laying on the floor toward the back of where the booth would have been was an engagement ring.

"It looks as if it might have slipped down in between the cushions where the benches meet," Danny said.

"Based on the fact that no one has been by looking for it, I assume the ring is no longer needed," I added.

"So are we thinking that Monica did or said something that resulted in a broken engagement?" Danny asked.

I nodded. "That's exactly what I'm thinking. I'd guess from where we just found it, the engagement was broken off while a couple was sitting in the booth. The woman must have taken off the ring and thrown it at the man, much the same way Monica threw her necklace at you. Maybe the woman stormed out and the man followed. The ring, forgotten, remained on the floor."

"Makes sense," Danny said. "So, given the fact that the cat most likely led you to the ring, not the phone number, do you suspect either the man or the woman is the one who killed Monica?"

"I would say it's a very good possibility. Now we just need to figure out who used to be engaged but no longer is."

"I can't think of anyone offhand," Danny said.

"Yeah, me neither, although I do remember a woman coming in and throwing something at Colin Cuthwright on Friday night. I didn't see what she threw and I don't remember if this is the booth where he was sitting. Let's bring it up to the gang. Did you ever talk to Colin?"

"I did. I don't have a good feeling for whether he might be the killer. He sure hated Monica. He said her actions brought a lot of grief to his grandfather, and he didn't deserve that. He was happy Monica was cut out of the will and not at all disappointed to find out she was dead. When I tried to dig a bit to find out if she might have had some information on him that he wouldn't want to be made public, he totally clammed up. I got the feeling he was hiding something, but I don't know what. He definitely didn't bring up an engagement."

"I think we should dig around some more. I still consider him the prime suspect. The cat did lead me to Francine's the other day, and the single piece of information I took from that conversation had to do with Monica's connection to the Cuthwright family and the lawsuit she filed against the estate and her cousins. We've pretty much proved Monica used her sexuality to trap and blackmail men on the island, so it isn't out of the realm of possibility that she had something on Colin that she was using as leverage. And Colin's tall and blond, so he fits the description of the mystery man in the parking lot. If this ring was thrown at him, that fits as well. I'll let Finn know about it. Maybe he can find out where it was purchased and who bought it."

"The bar is open tonight, so Aiden and I will be tied up here, but if you figure something out, call me on my cell."

"I will. And if you pick up a clue, call me as well."

******

Cassie and Tara wanted to come along with me to look at bride magazines with Siobhan, so it was four of us who met to scour the pages of the most popular ones. Siobhan had gone all out, offering us flutes of champagne and trays of finger foods and decadent desserts.

"Before we start narrowing down the design for the wedding dress, I have bridesmaid dresses I want to run by you." Siobhan handed me papers she'd printed off the internet with photos of very simple but elegant dresses. "The bodice of this one is fitted, the skirt hangs simply and is neither too full nor too narrow, and you can order it with or without straps. It also comes in five colors. I checked, and the store has our sizes in stock and can mail them out tomorrow with two-day shipping if we order by midnight."

"I like it." I passed the paper to Tara and Cassie. "What do you think?"

"It's a great dress," Cassie said.

"Simple yet elegant," Tara agreed.

"And we would all match without having to go to the hassle of finding custom-made bridesmaids' dresses," Siobhan added. "If you like this dress, we just need to decide on a color and I'll get them ordered."

Tara looked at me. "It's your wedding. What color would you like us to wear?"

I took the paper back and looked at it again. "The guys are all wearing black suits with white shirts and black ties. I'll be wearing a white dress. How about if we order the dresses in black? A black-and-white wedding would be simple yet elegant. And with a black dress, it's more likely you can wear it again for another occasion."

Siobhan hugged me. I had the feeling there was going to be a lot of hugging going on this evening. "I think black is great," she said. "I'll go order them while you start looking for a wedding dress design."

"Maybe I should just buy one of these in white. It's a perfectly lovely dress and I did want simple."

Siobhan shook her head. "No. Maggie is over-the-moon excited about making your dress, and I'm sure she'll make you something perfect. You're the bride; you should have something tailored exactly to your taste and mood."

"I don't disagree, but there isn't a lot of time to make a dress."

"Marley is on board to help," Siobhan said, referring to our aunt's best friend, "and when I spoke to Maggie today, she said she and Michael are going to stay on the island until after the wedding. In fact, they might stay through Thanksgiving. That way she can be part of the pre-wedding festivities and you'll be close by for fittings as she works. She really wants to do this. It's important to her."

My throat tightened with emotion. A dress made by Maggie and Marley would be magical. "Okay," I said. "Let's start designing."

"Remember," Siobhan said, "Maggie can make anything, so you aren't really looking for a dress but elements that would make up your perfect dress. Maggie will be most interested in what bodice you prefer and whether you'd like a full skirt or a straight one. Lace or no lace, train or no train. Things like that."

"Okay." I took a sip of my champagne. "I have an image in my head, but it'd be fun to look through the magazines for additional ideas. Are Maggie and Michael staying here at the house?"

"Yes. I told her when she gave us the house, her room would always be here, and I meant it. I know she's excited to see everyone, and she's really excited to spend some quality time with Connor. I've missed her."

I felt tears form in the corners of my eyes. "Yeah, me too."

By the end of the evening, Siobhan had taken all my ideas and drawn exactly what was in my head. I wasn't sure how many bottles of champagne we'd shared, but we most likely weren't going to get any sleuthing done this evening. We convinced Tara to stay overnight so she wouldn't have to drive home. I called Cody to let him know I'd be back in the cabin later than I expected, and he told me to have fun and he'd see me in the morning. Finn was hanging out with Danny and Aiden at the bar. I'd overheard a conversation between him and Siobhan earlier in the evening and it sounded like they were working on a new theory. Of course I also heard her tell Finn that to the extent I was involved, any talk of murder could wait until tomorrow. In retrospect, it was a good thing we'd taken a night off from our investigation because as it turned out, things were about to get serious.

Chapter 9

Wednesday, October 31

"Good morning, sunshine," Cody said the next morning as he gently nudged me awake. "I brought coffee and a breakfast sandwich."

I groaned as I stretched my arms over my head in an attempt to work the kinks from my body. "What time is it?"

"Ten fifteen."

My eyes flew open. "What!" I sat up and glanced at the bedside clock. "Damn," I said as I realized I was going to be very late for work.

"It's fine," Cody assured me. "Tara, Cassie, and Willow have things covered at the bookstore. I spoke to Tara, and she said you should plan to take the day off."

I tossed off the covers and slowly sat up. "I guess I must have had a bit too much champagne last night."

Cody laughed. "I'd say you had *a lot* too much champagne last night. But I'm glad you had fun. I would have let you sleep as long as you wanted, but Finn has been working on the case and he has a theory about who the killer might be. He's having trouble finding the evidence he needs, though, and wants to borrow Mystic."

"Mystic?"

Cody handed me a tall cup of coffee. "He wants me to bring both of you to his office at around eleven thirty."

I took a long sip of the hot black fluid. "Okay. Give me a minute to drink this and grab a shower." I looked around the room. "Where's Max? I would think he'd have woken me hours ago. He must need to go out."

"Rambler and I came by earlier. You were sleeping soundly, so Max joined us for a run. I fed him and Mystic as well."

I frowned. "I'm surprised I didn't hear you."

"You were sleeping pretty soundly. So, I take it you had fun last night?"

I nodded. "I had the best time. Siobhan and Tara helped me design a dress. Maggie and Michael are coming today so she can get to work. They're staying on the island until after Thanksgiving, which I'm superexcited about. I miss them both."

"That's great. It will be good to see them. Do you want this egg and bacon sandwich?"

I shook my head. "I don't think I'm up for food right now. Maybe after I get some coffee in me. I can't believe I drank so much. I never drink that much, but everyone kept toasting everything. We toasted when we ordered the bridesmaids dresses, we toasted once we had the concept for my dress down on paper, we toasted when the flower selection had been narrowed down." I put my hand on my stomach. "I wonder why everyone else isn't hung over."

"I'm sure they paced themselves. They wanted you to have fun. I think they planned to cover for you at work today all along. I'll stick this sandwich in the refrigerator. You can heat it up later if you want. Right now, you need to finish your coffee and get dressed. I'll call Finn to let him know we might be a few minutes late."

I'm not sure how I did it, but somehow I got up and stumbled into the shower. By the time I'd showered, dressed, eaten the egg sandwich, and drunk two more cups of coffee, I was feeling halfway human. I grabbed the cat carrier for Mystic and we headed into town. Maybe, I hoped, Finn's theory would work out and we'd have the person who killed Monica behind bars by the end of the day.

******

"You look like hell," Finn teased when we arrived at his office.

"Thank you very much. You're always such a charmer."

Finn laughed. "Seriously. I'm glad you had a good time last night, and I'm sorry I had to pull you away from what I'm sure was a perfectly lovely hangover."

"No problem. What do you need?"

"I've been working on the case while you were partying with the girls. First off I spoke to Danny who spoke with his beer distributer who confirmed that the earring you found belonged to her. She said she must have lost it when she delivered the new kegs the day before the opening. I suppose we'll never know why the crime scene guys didn't find it but we can cross it off our list of possible clues."

I stifled a yawn. "Well I guess that is one mystery solved."

Finn grinned. "Oh but there is more. I can now confirm Monica was, indeed, blackmailing the men she lured out to the house on the north shore and took photos of. I thought one of those men might be the killer, but after a bit of research, I've managed to clear everyone whose photo was in the envelope. I've settled on Colin Cuthwright as most likely the killer. The problem is, while I have a theory, I don't have any real proof."

"What do you know?"

Finn shifted a pile of files on his desk. He opened one and took out a photo of a very beautiful woman. I was sure it was the same one I'd seen in the bar. The same one who'd thrown something at Colin and then stormed out.

"I found out that after Colin received his inheritance and became a very rich man, the woman he'd been lusting after for the past two years and dating for the six months prior to their engagement, finally decided to commit to marrying him," Finn began. "Her name is Abigale Newman. Abigale is a model who lives in Los Angeles but works all over the world. From what I've been able to find out, Colin met Abigale at a photo shoot in Milan a couple of years ago and, according to friends, he fell for her hard, but she wasn't interested in a trust-fund baby who lived with his grandfather and who he depended on for his monthly allowance. It appears after Colin received his inheritance, Abigale had a change of heart."

"So if Monica had something on Colin, he might feel that whatever she had on him threatened his relationship," I supplied.

"That's exactly what I decided," Finn confirmed. "I continued to dig around and talk to Colin's friends. Most were pretty tight-lipped about both his relationship with Monica and Abigale, but after at least a dozen pretty useless interviews, I found one person who was willing to talk. He wanted to remain anonymous to avoid Colin's wrath, but he told me Monica claimed to have something on Colin she felt was valuable. She tried to use that knowledge to blackmail Colin into testifying on her behalf at the hearing on the inheritance. He was sure she was bluffing and refused. That made Monica very unhappy, so she tracked down Abigale as soon as she arrived on the island and provided her with whatever she had on Colin. The friend didn't know exactly what that was, but it seems it was enough to cause Abigale to break things off with Colin."

"I saw Abigale come in and throw something at Colin on Friday night. I bet it was the ring. She stormed out and he followed, but I know he came back because I saw him later in the evening."

"It would seem this broken engagement gives Colin a very strong reason to have entered into an altercation with Monica on the night she died."

"I agree," I said. "In addition to everything you just said, Mystic led me over to Francine's place. She was the one who filled me in on the whole inheritance thing. Plus, he's tall with blond hair, so he could very well be the mystery man from the parking lot. It really does look like he could be our guy." I paused to take a breath. "What do you need from us?"

"Proof that Monica tried to blackmail Colin. I figured if she had it with her on the island, which I suspect she did from the timetable of the murder, she most likely hid it in the house on the north shore where you found the photos she squirreled away. But I've searched the house from top to bottom and haven't found a thing. I'm hoping your cat will have better luck."

I glanced at Mystic, who was sprawled out in the sun on the floor near the window. "Okay. Mystic and I are willing to head up to the house to take a look around. Are you coming with us?"

Finn nodded.

******

The house looked as if it had been thoroughly tossed since Cody and I had been there. I took Mystic from the cat carrier and set him on the floor, then encouraged him to do his thing. His thing, I knew from past experience with magical cats, was to wander around and notice things, if there was anything worth noticing. The cat didn't spend a lot of time wandering around before he headed directly into the kitchen. Finn, Cody, and I followed to find him pawing at the pantry door. Finn opened the pantry and the cat wandered in, jumped up onto the top shelf, and began pawing at the plywood door leading to the crawl space above the room. Finn took down the plywood, then stood up on a stool to poke his head into the space. He reached a hand in and pulled out an envelope.

"Good job," I said to Mystic as Finn opened the envelope. "What did he find?" I asked.

"Photos of Colin with another man," Finn answered.

I scrunched up my nose. "Really? I thought he was engaged. To a woman," I emphasized.

"He was. These are old photos. Colin looks like a teenager in them."

"And the other man?" I asked.

Finn frowned. "I'm not sure. He's older. Quite a bit older, I think, but none of the photos show his face."

I wanted to look to see if I could make out the identity of the other man, but I also very much didn't want to look. "Are there any distinguishing characteristics?' I asked instead.

"The other man has a tattoo on his left shoulder. The photo is blurry, though, so I can't make out what it says. It seems to be a word, or maybe a series of words."

I tried to think whether I knew anyone who had a tattoo with a word printed on their shoulder but was coming up blank. If the photos had been taken when Colin was still a teenager, chances were the man could have left the island. "I guess you have what Monica was using to put pressure on Colin," I said. "These photos certainly would be damaging if they got out, and it seems they were enough to cause Colin's fiancée to change her mind about marrying him. I can see why Colin might have been mad enough to kill her. At this point we don't even know that the murder was intentional. She argued with someone and ended up dead due to blunt force trauma. It sounds like a crime of passion."

Finn slipped the photos back into the envelope. "Whether Monica's murder was premeditated or the result of impulse, I think I have enough now to bring Colin in. I'll drop the two of you off at Cody's truck and then track him down. And thanks." Mystic meowed and wound his way through Finn's legs. "Thanks to Mystic as well," Finn added.

Cody had some work to finish up at the newspaper, so he ran me back to my cabin after Finn dropped us off. He promised to come by when he'd finished what he was doing, but I had a few hours, so I decided to run into town and take care of some errands. After making a quick grocery list, I headed to Harthaven. The girls had suggested I stop in at the bakery and look at samples of wedding cakes. With the wedding less than three weeks away, there wasn't time to waste. After that, I wanted to run by the florist, and then the market. It worked out well that I had today off despite the headache I still hadn't gotten rid of. Maybe I'd stop by to say hi to my mom as well. I didn't want her to feel left out of things. And then I wanted to talk to Siobhan to see if she knew which ferry Maggie and Michael would be arriving on.

The florist came first on my route. All the wedding details were going to be tight, but I didn't need a lot of flowers and the ones I wanted to use were all common, so the florist thought she could fill my order without a problem. I let her know that my mother would be in to pay for them. After that, I headed to the bakery. What I hoped to do was look at the designs they had to offer. When it came to selecting a flavor, I wanted Cody to have some input, although I didn't think he'd care one way or another. Given the seasonal nature of the wedding, the girls and I had discussed a simple cake with white frosting and flowers in shades of red, orange, and yellow, a fall cake for a fall wedding.

"You should try their marble cake," someone said from behind me.

I turned around. "Edwin. What are you doing here?"

"Handing out flyers." Edwin held up a fistful of colorful posters I assumed he'd been pinning to bulletin boards. "I'm debating the other candidates for island council on Monday evening. We're hoping for a good turnout."

"I'll take a flyer to put up in the bookstore, but I'm not sure I'll be able to be there. How are things going with the campaign?"

"They're going really well. Oh, there have been a few road bumps along the way, but things seem to be back on track now. I heard you and Cody have set a date for your wedding."

"We have. Word travels fast."

"I was in the florist before this. I was happy to hear you'd been in selecting flowers. I've been pulling for the two of you. I honestly thought you might have gotten together when you were in high school, but I guess I was just reading things wrong back then. Still, I was happy to hear you finally found each other."

"I guess you remember my brother Danny was Cody's best friend in high school. I think back then I was just the pesky little sister."

"I had both Cody and Danny in class. Now that I think about it, I remember you were a couple of years younger. Still, despite the delay, it's nice to see that nature makes sure things work out as they should in the end."

"Yes, it is nice when that happens." I glanced at the clock on the wall. "I need to run. Good luck with your campaigning."

"Before you go—" Edwin stopped me. "I heard Finn was back on the murder case. Have you heard anything?"

I shook my head. "Not really. I think he has a suspect in mind, but you know everything is pretty top secret until an arrest is made."

"So he's close to an arrest?"

"I'm really not sure."

"I see. I thought maybe you'd been working with him, as you often do."

"I was helping out, but I have a lot of wedding stuff to see to today. Listen, I really need to run." I held up the flyer. "I'll try to swing by on Monday."

As I left the bakery, I had the oddest feeling I knew something important I couldn't quite bring to the surface. I supposed it could just be my hangover messing with my head. I paused on the sidewalk and looked back toward the bakery. Edwin was still inside, but he was looking in my direction. I felt a chill run up my spine as I turned and continued down the sidewalk toward the produce stand where I liked to shop for fresh fruits and vegetables when I was in Harthaven. I'd known Edwin a long time and genuinely enjoyed chatting with him. I had no idea where the uneasy feeling I was experiencing came from, but it was very real. Maybe our discussion had ignited a memory or a suppressed thought. I'd definitely had that experience before.

As I picked out a selection of fruits and vegetables, I forced myself to think back. At what point had I begun to feel uneasy? I guess it was when Edwin was talking about having Cody, Danny, and me in his class. He hadn't been my favorite teacher, but I didn't remember having a negative opinion of him. He liked to ramble on and on, even when he was standing in front of a room full of students conducting a lecture. And he'd had some really odd opinions when the class discussed World War II. And then I remembered. I knew I'd seen a man with a word tattooed on his shoulder before. Edwin Brown had the word—or rather several words: *Arbeit macht frei.* I remembered the term had been used in relation to labor and death camps and translated to *work sets you free.*

"Edwin was the man with Colin," I whispered, reaching for my phone as I did.

"I was wondering if you'd seen the photos," said a voice from behind me as a hand clamped over my mouth, and the world began to fade to black.

Chapter 10

"You killed Monica," I said when I came to. I was tied up in the back of Edwin's car. We were heading toward the northeast side of the island as far as I could tell. "Why?"

"She was going to publish the photos she stole from my home. I couldn't have that. It would have ruined my reputation. A reputation, I'll remind you, I've spent a lifetime creating."

I wanted to wipe the hair from in front of my eyes, but my hands were tied behind my back. "It was you with Colin." I paused to try to clear the remainder of the fog from my brain. "He was just a kid. A teenager."

"He knew what he was doing."

"There were others," I realized.

Edwin didn't answer. I shook my head in an attempt to dislodge my hair from my face. "You do know that it is morally and legally wrong for a grown man to have relations with minors?"

"Thus my need to recover the photos at any cost."

I was sure I was going to be sick. "Photos? Why on earth would you take photos?" I put my hand to my mouth. "Forget that. Anyone sick enough to seduce his students would be sick enough to take photos of the whole thing." I looked out the window at the passing landscape. "Where are we going anyway?"

"Not important."

"Are you going to kill me too?"

I noticed Edwin glance into the rearview mirror. "I don't want to, but I'm afraid you've left me no choice."

"You always have a choice."

"No," Edwin said with such force it made me cringe. "You don't always have a choice."

Okay, there was definitely a story behind that statement. I was willing to bet there was a story behind his tattoo as well. I decided that reasoning with him wasn't going to get me anywhere, so I turned my focus to trying to find a way out of the mess I'd suddenly found myself in.

When we arrived at a house, I saw a boat tied up at a nearby dock. Fantastic, I thought, when I realized he probably planned to escape on the boat, avoiding the ferry altogether. I wasn't sure if he planned to kill me before he took off in his getaway boat or if he planned to bring me along as a hostage. Either way, I had the feeling I was never going to have my chance at a life with Cody if I didn't figure a way out of this fast.

"You aren't old enough to have fought in World War II, so I have to assume the tattoo on your shoulder is to remind you of a situation you experienced that brings to mind the helplessness and hopelessness of being imprisoned."

"How do you know about the tattoo?"

"The end-of-the-school-year picnic when I was a sophomore. We were at the beach and Lenora Patterson swam too far out and began to panic. You dove in and rescued her. Before you did, you took off your T-shirt. I noticed the tattoo and was curious about what it meant, so I wrote it down and looked it up later. To be honest, that was so long ago I'd totally forgotten about it. Until today, that is."

Edwin stopped the car and turned off the engine. "The story behind my tattoo is no concern of yours. Let's just say my life went down a very different path from yours." He opened the driver's side door and got out. Then he opened the door to the back seat where I was sitting. "Now get out."

I didn't figure I had a lot of choice right then, so I did. I hoped we'd walk to the house, but instead he shoved me toward the boat. Being held captive in the house would at least have afforded me a chance of escape; the boat, not so much.

"Are we going somewhere?" I asked.

"We are."

"Can I at least use the bathroom first?"

Edwin paused.

"Please. Siobhan threw me a pre-wedding party last night and I'm afraid I drank too much. The ride out here has made my already fragile stomach even more upset. I think I might puke."

Edwin frowned but still didn't answer.

I decided to take a page from Mystic's book and started dry heaving.

"Okay. Come with me. The bathroom is this way."

Edwin gave me a shove toward the house. I stumbled along, continuing to heave. "I'll need my hands," I said after we entered the house.

He hesitated.

"If I don't have my hands, I'll probably puke all over the floor. And there's more."

"More?"

"There might be something going on at the other end too."

Edwin cringed as I glanced at my backside. I could tell he wasn't thrilled about the situation, but he cut my hands free before he shoved me into the bathroom and closed the door behind me. I realized I was going to have to make some gross sounds in case he was listening, so I continued to pretend I was hurling up the contents of my stomach while I looked around for a way out. I'd hoped the bathroom would have a window, but no such luck. Eventually, my fake puking was going to cease to distract him and he'd haul me out of the room and onto the boat as he'd planned. I needed more time.

"Are you almost done in there?" Edwin demanded from the other side of the door.

"I don't suppose you have any tampons?" I improvised.

"No, I don't. Figure out a way to deal with everything that's coming out of your body so we can get out of here. You have two minutes."

Two minutes wasn't a lot, but it did give me a minute to look around.

"Ew, gross," I called out as I began opening drawers and cupboards.

"Is something wrong?" Edwin called out.

"There's just some really nasty stuff coming out of me. Trust me, you don't want to come in here. I'm going to look for something to use to clean myself up." I figured if he heard me opening drawers and cupboards, I'd just provided a plausible explanation why. I knew Edwin was a lifelong bachelor, so I was pretty sure he wasn't prepared to deal with whatever might be happening on my side of the door.

A complete search of the bathroom didn't provide me with any objects that could be used as a weapon, but I did find a can of Lysol with bleach. Well, it was better than nothing. Edwin had overpowered me and used something over my face to cause me to pass out, but I hadn't seen a gun. I was banking on him not having one. After a brief pause to gather my courage, I took the cap off the spray can, flushed the toilet again for good measure, and called out that I was finished. When the door opened I sprayed the Lysol directly into Edwin's eyes, then ran as fast as I could out the door and toward the drive. I'd made it to the street when I heard Edwin cursing me from the doorway of the house. I just kept running, hoping to find a place to hide before he came after me in the car.

There weren't a lot of options for hiding places. I figured that unless I saw somewhere that might provide me a good chance of not being seen, continuing to run was my best option. Right about the time my lungs began to burn, I could hear a car behind me. I hated to pause to turn around, so I just kept running, but I realized there was a good chance it was Edwin. I was about to head for the water to try to swim for it when I saw Finn's car coming toward me from the other direction.

******

As it turned out, the clerk from the produce market had seen Edwin force me into his car. He'd called Finn, who'd called Cody, who managed to track down an address for Edwin. Both men had come after me. It was a good thing I'd faked all the bodily discharge. If I hadn't, Edwin would have been out to sea and I most likely would have been dead before Finn got to us.

"So Colin turned out to be both involved and uninvolved in Monica's murder," Cody said to me later that evening as we sat on the swing on my deck and looked out toward the sea.

I nodded. "According to Finn, Colin was completely fed up with his cousin after she told his fiancée that the two of them were actually kissing cousins who did a lot more than kiss and had been at it like dogs in heat since she'd been back on the island. It wasn't true, but apparently Colin has lied to his fiancée in the past so she decided to believe Monica. When Edwin confessed to Colin on the night of the opening that he'd argued with Monica about the photos of his rendezvous with his students all those years ago and in the process he'd killed her, Colin agreed not to say anything."

"So was it him in the parking lot after the murder?" Cody asked.

"Finn said yes. I guess Colin wanted to see how the whole thing played out."

"And Monica?" Cody asked. "Did Colin know why she'd been acting so crazy since she'd been on the Island?"

I leaned back and let out a small sigh. "No. Colin was as confused by Monica's crazy behavior as everyone else. I don't suppose we'll ever really know what was going on. Her behavior started before she ever came to the island. I suppose that she could have suffered an event in her life that sent her completely over the edge."

Cody put his arm around my shoulders and pulled me closer. "I'm just glad it is over. I could have lost you today if Mystic's fake puking hadn't saved your life."

I laughed. "The cat is a freaking genius. We have to find him the perfect home."

"You could just keep him," Cody suggested.

"No. It's not that I wouldn't love to, but that's not the way it works. The cats come to me to help me solve the problem I'm faced with, and I find them the home they're meant to live in for the rest of their lives. I'm sure Mystic has a destiny, the same as the other cats. It might take a day or two to reveal itself, but I'm sure it will."

Cody kissed the top of my head. "I'm sure you're right. I'm sorry your dinner plans with your family had to be put on hold so you could give your statement to the man who came over from the sheriff's office."

"I spoke to Aunt Maggie briefly. She understood. And she's going to be here until after Thanksgiving, so there'll be plenty of time to get together. I'm sorry that between my kidnapping and Edwin's arrest and my part in it that I wasted my entire day off. I never even finished looking at wedding cakes."

"How about if you and I go do that tomorrow?"

"I'd love that. After I decided to look at cakes, I realized I should have waited for you. Now that we've committed to having the wedding in November, I'm beginning to feel a little manic about getting everything done."

"We'll get it done," Cody assured me. "We both want to keep it simple. As long as we don't lose sight of that, we'll be fine."

"I agree." I closed my eyes as the cool night air brushed my face. It was so cozy being snuggled up with Cody in front of the fire while the waves rolled onto the beach. "I'm really going to miss this."

"There's a beach at Mr. Parsons's house."

"True, but there isn't a deck with a swing just steps from the water."

"We could build one. In fact, we could build a guest cottage exactly like this one. Only instead of using it for guests, it could be our own private hideaway. At least until we have children."

I smiled. "I like that idea. It would be nice to have a place to sneak away to that's just ours. I even thought about keeping this cabin, but I've given it more thought, and it's definitely time to hand it down to Cassie. I mentioned it to Siobhan last night and she loved the idea."

"Is Cassie quitting college?" Cody asked.

"I haven't asked her, but it seems to be where she's heading. In the long term, she'll need to figure out her own path, but in the short term, we can use her help at the bookstore."

"Cassie likes to write and is good with computers. I could use her help at the newspaper too if she's interested."

"If she does decide to quit college, I think you should ask her. In the meantime, you should know that, while I was feeling the effects of too much alcohol and too much almost dying earlier in the day, I'm actually feeling much better now that I've had a chance to unwind a bit."

Cody raised a brow. "Enough better?"

I leaned forward and kissed Cody firmly on the lips. "Definitely enough better."

Chapter 11

Thursday, November 1

"I'd like to make a toast," Aiden said after standing at the end of the table where he sat next to my mother. "To my little sister Cait, who can't seem to stay out of trouble, and the man who always seems to find a way to save her, my almost-brother, Cody."

The entire family plus a few honorary others had gathered to celebrate the fact that Cody and I had finally set a date and to welcome Aunt Maggie and her new husband, Michael Kilian, to the island for a nice long visit. It was a good thing the house Maggie had given Finn and Siobhan had a large dining room; there were fourteen of us gathered around the table.

"Did you and Cody pick out a cake today?" Siobhan asked while she juggled eating her meal with feeding Connor, who was in a high chair.

"We did: a white cake with fall flowers. I think it's going to be beautiful."

"I'd like to find a day to go to Seattle to find a dress," my mom said.

"I'll go with you," Maggie offered. "If you want to go tomorrow, I can pick up what I need for Cait's dress as well."

"I'm glad you were able to settle on dresses for the bridesmaids so easily," Marley said. "That can sometimes turn into a major project."

"We're most definitely keeping things simple," I said, giving Cody's hand a squeeze under the table. "In fact, I think planning our Thanksgiving feast at Mr. Parsons's is going to turn out to be more labor-intense than planning the wedding."

"It's a lot of work. Are you sure you want to do it?" Mom asked.

"I'm sure. It means a lot to Mr. Parsons. He's really looking forward to it. We may end up with twice the number of guests I originally planned on once he finishes inviting everyone he has in mind, but it's so nice to see him so happy."

"The biggest challenge I can see is cooking so many turkeys all at once," Siobhan said.

"I'm going to precook the turkeys and then just heat the meat on the day of the party. It isn't ideal, but we're going to need your kitchen, Mr. Parsons's kitchen, Francine's kitchen, and my kitchen, just to handle all the sides. I thought I'd assign different sides to each of the kitchens we plan to use."

"Smart," Siobhan said as the conversation moved on to the subject of pies and rolls.

Being part of a large family could be challenging, but at times like this, when we all came together with a common goal in mind, working with people I both loved and had been a part of me my entire life was more precious than I could describe.

"It looks like there's someone in the drive," Cassie said.

I glanced out the window. "I have a feeling that may be the man I spoke to today about Mystic." I stood up. "I'll just be a minute."

I'd had a call earlier in the day from someone who was looking for a gentle animal to act as a therapy cat for a ten-year-old girl who was the only survivor of a house fire in which her entire family died. The man, her uncle, had taken over as guardian for the girl, who was so traumatized she refused to speak. He hoped having a gentle animal for her to bond with would help her along the road to recovery. I told the man we had many cats to choose from, including kittens, but I also mentioned I had a specific cat in mind who I thought would be just perfect.

The man parked and got out of the car, then walked around and opened the passenger door. A thin girl with straight brown hair climbed out of the vehicle.

"This is Naomi," the man said.

"Hi, Naomi. My name is Cait. I have a lot of cats you can look at if you'd like, but I have a very special cat who needs a very special home. His name is Mystic. Would you like to meet him?"

The girl nodded.

"Okay, let's go over to my cabin."

I led the girl and her uncle to the cabin. I opened the door and called to Mystic, who wandered out onto the deck. The minute the cat and the girl locked eyes with each other, I could see it was love at first sight on both sides. The girl bent down and the cat approached. He began to purr so loudly, the sound permeated the night air.

"What do you think?" the uncle asked. "Would you like to take Mystic home with you?"

The girl nodded.

"I guess you have a special home for your special cat. How much do I owe you?"

"Oh, there's no charge," I said. "I'm just happy Mystic found his human. Let me give you some food and a few supplies to get you started."

Once the man's trunk had been loaded up with everything he'd need, I watched him drive away with the cat I had come to care for in the past week. Letting the cats go at the end of their duty was always difficult, though it also felt right.

"Are you okay?" Cody walked up behind me. He put his arms around my waist and pulled me back against his chest.

"I am. Better than okay. It's been a dicey week, but things seem to have worked out well."

Cody kissed my neck. "It's nice having everyone together for dinner again. I miss those big Sunday meals at your mother's."

"Yeah. Me too. I used to complain about them, but now that Mom no longer has a house and doesn't cook the meals, I miss them. Gabe has a big kitchen and dining area. Maybe when he and Mom get married, she'll start doing Sunday dinner again."

"Have they set a date?"

"Mom said something about spring or summer. I think she wants to be sure Cassie is settled before she takes such a big step."

"I can understand that. Did you talk to Cassie about school and the cabin?"

"Not yet. My sense is that she's still thinking things over. I don't want to influence her by giving her the cabin yet. Once she makes her decision, we can talk about it. In the meantime, it can be our love nest."

Cody chuckled. "That sounds like a very good plan to me."

I turned around so I was facing Cody. I put my arms around his neck, leaned forward, and kissed him. "I guess we should go back in."

"Yeah. I guess we should."

"But later," I said against his lips.

"Later and forever after." Cody deepened the kiss and the world faded away.

Bonus Short Story

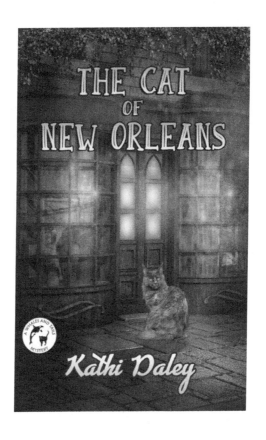

The Cat of New Orleans

A Whales and Tails Mini Mystery

New Orleans

If I hadn't been so preoccupied with lingering thoughts of death, I might have enjoyed the throngs of people, deafening music, bright lights, and pungent scents. If I hadn't been driven to the point of exhaustion, I might have better tolerated the stifling heat that felt like a wool blanket swaddling me with itchy dampness. If I hadn't been dealing with the knot in my stomach, brought on by overwhelming fear and a sense of hopelessness, I might have found the sheer energy of the place to be intoxicating rather than overwhelming.

"Are you sure this is the right place?" I asked my fiancé, Cody West, as I stepped over a man who had passed out on the sidewalk just inches from the busy street where cars and pedestrians competed for the same piece of roadway.

"According to the note Devalinda left, we're to meet our contact at La Fleur Noire at eleven o'clock. According to the GPS on my phone, we should find the bar about halfway down the next block."

"I hope our contact isn't late. This," I swept my hand in a circular motion, "all if this, is a lot more than I'm able to process. I'm really not sure how much more of this I can tolerate."

"I know. It's a lot to take in. Once we get the map we can head back to an air-conditioned room and a cold shower."

I took a deep breath and nodded, wishing all the while I was home on my island off the coast of Washington State, where the temperatures were mild and the humidity tolerable. When Cody had suggested I come with him to New Orleans for a romantic vacation when he was asked to speak about the training program he'd developed for new SEAL recruits on a local network talk show, I'd enthusiastically agreed. Little did I know our romantic interlude would quickly turn into a sort of crazy scavenger hunt to find a map leading to a stone that had been purported to possess the power to restore the magic that seemed to be linked to my witchy friend Tansy. While I didn't really understand the specifics, based on what Tansy's life partner, Bella, had told me, if the magic on Madrona Island died, Tansy would as well.

"I don't think it's much farther," Cody assured me as we wove our way through the crowd that seemed to suck the air from my surroundings as additional bodies pushed onto the narrow sidewalk.

I let out a little screech as someone bumped into me, spilling a blue daiquiri down the front of my shirt. I momentarily considered belting the guy, but Cody grabbed my hand and pulled me forward through the mass of people, most of whom appeared to be drunk. One more hour, I told myself. One more clandestine meeting in a dark and dank alley. One more stressful encounter with people I couldn't relate to and or understand. One more task to complete before I could claw my way out of the *Caitlin Hart in Wonderland* nightmare I'd fallen into and put the most absurd day I'd ever experienced behind me.

"I think we'll need to cross the street," Cody said, taking my hand. "Be careful. The drivers in this part of town don't seem to care if they run you down."

I nodded tiredly and followed along. Could this day get any worse?

Actually, I admitted, as I bounced helplessly like a pinball off one person and into another, the day had started off all right. The show Cody was in town to tape had aired early that morning, leaving us plenty of time, we thought, to take in the sights and partake of some down-home Cajun food before we took care of the errand we'd promised to carry out for Tansy. Cody had been confident and prepared and the interview went perfectly. He spent a half hour receiving thanks and congratulations from the staff at the small television station, then we set off into what promised to be a hot, sunny day. We hadn't even made it to the first stop on our list of touristy things to do, though, when I received a call from Bella with a plea that I move up the timeline to retrieve the magical stone that was supposed to restore the magic on Madrona Island and save Tansy's life. When Tansy had asked me to fetch the stone, she hadn't attached any element of urgency to the request, so we planned to complete the task at our leisure, but, according to Bella, the time for urgency had actually come and passed.

My task was to pick up the stone from Tansy's friend Jasmina, who apparently was some sort of a priestess with mystical powers I can't claim to understand. She lived deep in the bayou, where the dense cover of trees, thick with Spanish moss, blocks the heat of the summer sun. Originally, our instruction from Tansy was to meet another friend of hers, a magic shop owner named Devalinda, near the French Quarter, later this evening. She, Tansy assured us, would provide us with a map, which would lead us to the guide who would take us to a small house deep in the bayou, where Jasmina lived. When Bella called now, however, she informed us that Devalinda couldn't see us as planned, so we needed to go to a different magic shop on another dingy corner and talk to a woman named Drusilla about the map. I figured one magic shop was the same as another, and we had a half hour before we were to meet with Tansy's contact, so I agreed to the change.

Of course, things are never as easy as they sound.

"This is it," Cody said, pausing outside a very crowded bar.

The music seeping from the interior of La Fleur Noire wasn't at all what I expected. It was deep and sensuous, with an alluring beat that touched your soul, drawing you into its hypnotic power despite any resistance you thought you might have had. Upon entering the dark room, we found it to be packed with men and women draped around each other in some sort of orgy simulation, although everyone was fully dressed. Well, sort of. There were a few women who barely wore enough to be defined as being fully dressed. With the heat, though, who could blame them?

"What are you drinking?" A tall, thin man with dark skin, dark hair, and dark eyes, gazed at me with such an intent stare that I found myself trying to look away.

"We're looking for Eden," Cody answered as I tried to break away from the man's gaze. "Devalinda sent us."

"Top of the stairs and to the right."

Cody thanked the man, then pulled me after him. While I'd been decidedly hot and sweaty before entering the bar, since entering it, I'd been drawn into the primal beat of the music and was becoming hot and sweaty in an entirely different way.

"Are you sure this is a good idea?" I asked as Cody led me through the writhing bodies on the dance floor toward the stairs.

"I'm pretty sure it's a terrible idea. Do you have a better one?"

"Other than going to the hotel for a cold shower, a cold drink, and a hot fiancé, not really."

"Just a few more minutes." Cody squeezed my hand.

After we reached the second floor we headed down the hallway to a room with long strands of beads from floor to ceiling where a door should have been. Should we knock? I didn't see how. Cody apparently had the same thought because he drew back the beads and walked in. The walls of the room were painted a dark purple that contrasted nicely with the plush carpet in a soft mauve. There was a small white sofa, which was flanked by white chairs in front of a fireplace made of white brick. Given the stifling heat of the day, I couldn't imagine it ever being cool enough to want to enjoy a crackling fire here, but perhaps for a few months out of the year.

The most interesting thing in the room, I decided, were the black flowers displayed in white vases on almost every surface. I supposed they were fitting: La Fleur Noire translated to The Black Flower in English.

Cody and I stood there for maybe thirty seconds before a tiny woman with straight black hair down to her waist floated in, a large brown cat following her.

"Eden?" Cody asked, as I realized the cat was the same one we'd been seeing all day.

The woman nodded and gestured with her hand for us to take a seat on the sofa. I glanced at Cody, and he nodded, so I followed his lead and did so.

"You have come for the map," the woman said with a deep voice bearing a strong Creole accent.

"Yes," Cody answered. "Devalinda sent us to fetch it."

Eden glided across the room, then sat down on a coffee table across from where we were sitting on the sofa. She faced me, then took both my hands in hers. She turned them over so they were palms up. "You are a keeper of the magic."

I glanced at Cody. He shrugged. I responded. "I assume you're talking about the cats." Back home on

Madrona Island, I, for reasons unbeknownst to me, had been entrusted with the role of working with the magical cats who helped me solve the endless mysteries that seemed to fall into my lap.

Eden didn't speak. She let go of my hands and then put her hands on my cheeks. She looked deeply into my blue eyes with eyes so dark you couldn't differentiate the pupil from the iris. I guess she must have been satisfied with what she saw there, because she got up, crossed the room, and then took an envelope from the drawer of what appeared to be a small desk. She returned and handed it to me. "Baptiste will meet you at the spot designated on the map at ten o'clock tomorrow night."

"Night?" I almost screeched. I wasn't at all thrilled about the idea of venturing into the bayou during the day, but I definitely wasn't prepared to go into a swamp teeming with alligators and snakes after dark.

Eden didn't respond to me, instead floating out of the room as effortlessly as she'd arrived. Cody and I paused for a moment, then let ourselves out. Once free of the allure of La Fleur Noire, we headed back through the crowded city toward the sanctity of our air-conditioned hotel.

"Did you notice the cat with Eden?" I asked as we set off down the street.

"It looked like the same cat we've been seeing all day."

"That's what I thought. I know it was at the magic shop and the police station, and I'm sure I saw it in the alley near the butcher shop. It was lingering in the background at the gallery as well."

"I guess it might be linked to this crazy journey we're taking," Cody said.

I thought back, trying to remember if I had, indeed, seen the cat in each location I'd mentioned. After Cody's interview we'd headed to Drusilla's magic shop. I remember walking into the store and being momentarily intrigued by all the items displayed on the shelves and countertops. There had been a cat sitting on one of the counters, and I saw it jump down and go up the stairs. I'd instinctively followed it. At the top of the stairs was a hallway. I saw the cat slip into a room with an open door, and I followed it to find two police officers standing over a puddle of blood. I later learned that blood was believed to have belonged to the shop owner, who'd been reported missing. Once the police officers noticed I looked a whole lot like the voodoo doll lying in the puddle of blood, Cody and I were escorted to the police station, where we were interviewed by a dark-skinned man who introduced himself as Officer Despre.

I didn't remember seeing the cat there until after the interview, but I couldn't forget the irritation I'd felt as the man took his sweet time asking us the same questions over and over again. No, I didn't know why the doll, which had long curly hair like mine, also happened to be wearing a shirt that looked almost identical to the one I'd chosen to wear today. And no, I didn't know how anyone would even know the color of the shirt I'd be wearing, unless they had been at the television station that morning. And finally, no, I didn't know why anyone, would take the time to make a doll, that everyone could see, had been created to look like me.

It was at the police station that our crazy day really took off. As our visit there rounded the two-hour mark, I was offered the chance to visit the ladies' room, which I took. Officer Despre pointed to the hallway and told me it was the third door on the left. I was just passing the second door on the right when the cat darted past me. I remembered it from the magic shop and followed it until a tall woman in a police uniform pulled me into what looked to be a file room. Before I could utter a word, she put a piece of paper into my hand, whispered what sounded like a curse in a language I didn't understand, then shoved me out into the hallway. I shrugged my shoulders, continued to the ladies' room, then stopped to read the note there.

Lafitte's at four. Order a General Jackson.

I'd stuck the note in my pocket, quickly refreshed myself, and returned to the interrogation room, where Cody waited with Officer Despre. When we were finally free to go I showed Cody the note.

"There's a bar called Lafitte's Blacksmith Shop Bar," Cody informed me. "It's on Bourbon Street."

As instructed, we'd arrived at Lafitte's at four o'clock. And there was what I was sure was the same cat I'd seen in the magic shop and the police station, sitting on top of the bar. I wondered if I should interact with it in some way, but the note hadn't said anything about it, so we sat down on two of the stools and ordered General Jacksons. We were served icy drinks in Styrofoam cups. On the bottom of mine was a name and address, which led us to a narrow alley in a seedy part of the city. I wasn't sure which of the deteriorating doors I should knock on until the same cat we'd been seeing all day appeared again and led us to the door of what we thought was a butcher shop. At least I hoped it was a butcher shop, because there was blood on the apron of the man who answered the door, as well as on the floor inside. The smell of death and decay was overwhelming. I honestly didn't think I'd be able to go very far into the stifling interior. Fortunately, the man seemed to know who we were and why we were there, and immediately gave us a note directing us to an art gallery featuring local art in the French Quarter.

In the gallery, a quick look through the window revealed an eclectic collection of art depicting New Orleans, the bayous, and colorful art with what I thought must be a voodoo theme. The gallery was appropriately called Laveau's, and it was closed when we arrived, though a woman was cleaning inside. I wondered whether the owner had hired a woman as a janitor, but the bright colors and fine fabric of the woman's light, airy dress, and the cat that was following her around suggested she might be the owner herself, and the person we were there to meet. We knocked on the door and she waved us in. She introduced herself before offering us a brief tour.

"I'd love one," I'd said before Cody could say something that might ruin my chance to spend some time in the interior of an air-conditioned building.

"The art in the main gallery is really different," Cody had responded. "Almost sensual but not overtly."

"Tish is a very talented artist. Come with me. I have more of her stuff in the back."

The art in the gallery moved me in a way I didn't quite understand. One oil painting of an old plantation house had me shedding an actual tear.

"You look like her," the gallery owner had said.

"Her?" I'd asked.

"The mistress of the house." She picked up a book and turned to a page which featured a photograph of a couple standing in front of the house. "This is the owner and his young wife."

I'm pretty sure my heart stopped beating at that point. I'm still not sure how I knew it, but when I looked at the photo, the man's name tumbled from my lips. "Pierre."

"Yes," she said with a smile. "I see you're familiar with the history of the house. Pierre Beaumont married Fiona Murphy in 1898. It was quite the scandal because Pierre was a wealthy man with a French heritage and Fiona was an Irish immigrant without a penny to her name."

I glanced at Cody. He hadn't said anything, but the frown on his face spoke volumes.

"They had a baby," I said, almost without realizing I had spoken. "A girl. Abigail."

"That's right," she confirmed. "Fiona got sick and died shortly after the baby's birth. Pierre tried to raise her on his own, but he was so overcome with grief that he eventually gave the baby to her maternal grandmother to raise."

"Grand-mère," I'd whispered.

"That's right. Although Pierre felt he couldn't raise the child on his own, he provided for her financially, and Abigail went on to attend college. She never married and died young, but she published several novels before her death that are actually quite good."

"Are the books still in print?" I asked.

"No. But you can find copies of them in the local library and museum. Are you a writer?"

"No, but I co-own a bookstore: Coffee Cat Books. It's actually a bookstore combined with a coffee bar and a cat lounge."

The woman smiled. "It sounds delightful."

"If you ever make it to Madrona Island in Washington State, be sure to stop by."

"I will. And do check out the novels. I think you'll find them very revealing."

I promised I would and she continued the tour. By the time it was over I'd cooled off a bit and felt much better prepared for whatever came next. I thanked the woman as she handed me yet another note, this one appearing to have been written by Devalinda, the witchy friend Tansy had directed us to in the first place. It led us to Eden at La Fleur Noire, which brings you up to the present.

"Cody," I said after we'd been quiet for several minutes.

"Yeah?"

"Don't you think it's odd that both the voodoo doll in the magic shop and the woman in the photo looked an awful lot like me?"

His arm tightened around my shoulders as we left the congestion of the French Quarter behind. "Yes, I do. What I think is even stranger was that you knew the name of the man in the photo even before the gallery owner said it to us."

I frowned. "The name popped into my head and escaped my lips almost before I formed the thought. I might have seen the photo before, or read about the couple somewhere, but I don't think that's it."

"You think you had a vision?"

I shook my head. "More like a memory."

Cody didn't respond. Not that I blamed him. I mean really, what was there to say? I know there are people who believe in things like reincarnation, but I'm Catholic born and raised and I can guarantee you, it's nowhere in our beliefs. I decided to change the subject to something with less of a *Twilight Zone* feel to it. "I spoke to Bella while you checked in with the newspaper and asked her about the voodoo doll. She said that although Drusilla practices voodoo, she has nothing to do with dolls, so she has no idea why one would be found in her shop. She also didn't know what was up with the blood and hadn't heard from the police herself, but she did say the doll could be a warning of some sort and we should tread carefully as we searched for the stone."

"Did Bella say how Tansy's doing?"

I bowed my head. "Not well. We need to restore the magic to the island before it's too late."

Cody and I crossed the street and entered the air-conditioned hotel lobby. He pushed the button for the elevator and we waited. He took my hand in his and gave it a squeeze. "Don't worry. We'll follow the map, find Jasmina, get the stone, and restore both the island's magic and Tansy's health."

I couldn't quite quell the hollowness in my soul. "I hope so."

"You'll feel better after a cool shower," Cody reassured me.

Alone in the elevator, I wrapped my arms around his neck, leaned forward, and captured his lips with mine. "A cool shower sounds great, but with the air-conditioning and all, I'm thinking we might need a way to warm back up."

He pulled me hard against his body. "I'm sure we can come up with a way to meet all your needs."

The Bayou

The heavy cloak of night settled around us as the light from the moon vanished beneath the heavy veil of the dense trees that grew in the area. My mind shifted to the chorus of sounds so foreign to my ears, I couldn't pick one out from another. A splash to my left reminded me that even under this cloak of darkness, the bayou teemed with life: beautiful, exotic, deadly.

"Hold up," Cody said as a large snake that had been hiding in the tall grass slithered slowly across our path.

"Oh God," I whispered as I grabbed Cody's arm and hung on tight. "I'm pretty sure my worst nightmare involves that snake."

"He's no more interested in picking a fight with us than we are in picking one with him. Just give him some space to move into the darkness. I think the light from my flashlight might have disturbed his nap."

I wanted to look away until he was gone, but somehow my eyes locked on to his slow, deliberate movements. He didn't seem to be paying us a bit of attention, but I couldn't help but be reminded of a patient hunter waiting and watching for the perfect moment to strike.

"He really is beautiful," I whispered.

"Beautiful but deadly. We need to watch where we step."

I looked around at the inky blackness. "It's kind of hard to do that when it's so dark. How much farther do we have to go until we're supposed to meet up with Baptiste?"

Cody took out the map and looked at the directions. "It's hard to tell. I've been trying to compare this map we received from Eden with a topographical map of the bayou I downloaded from the internet and the two aren't lining up."

"Well, that's not good. Do you think Eden's map is wrong?"

Cody shook his head. "No. The map she gave us is just different from the other one. For example, see this area here, where the river makes an S through this grove of cypress?"

I looked at the map Cody shone his flashlight on. "Yes, I see it."

"We passed it about five minutes ago."

"We did?" Five minutes ago I'd been watching as the long, knobby length of an alligator slowly made its way just beneath the surface of the murky water that lined the narrow path we were traveling on either side. "I guess I was distracted."

"It's easy to lose your focus when you're in an unfamiliar environment, but it's best to keep an eye out. There are all sorts of things out here we'll want to be aware of."

I swallowed hard. Snakes, alligators, and bobcats. What was I thinking?

"I think it's safe for us to continue," Cody said as he took a tentative step forward.

"Cody," I said as I took a step to follow.

"Yeah?"

"Was this what it was like for you when you were with the SEAL team?"

He turned and looked back at me. "I guess. In a way. I never had to make my way through a bayou, but I did have missions that took me into hot jungles that had a similar feel. Of course, most of my missions were in the desert, and when I was with the SEALs I was part of a team. It was different because I knew we could all take care of ourselves, so I only had myself to worry about."

"You don't need to worry about me. I can take care of myself," I shot back, even though at least in this situation we both knew I'd have been alligator bait by now if Cody hadn't been with me.

"You are very capable," Cody diplomatically agreed.

I wanted to make a remark about the capable label, but it was too hot and I was too tired. Being moody and unreasonable was a lot of work, and I knew it was better to conserve my strength. As the heavy air threatened to suffocate me, I tried to focus on Cody's back rather than the darkness all around me. Shapes outlined in the shadows seemed to whisper in the muggy night as we made our way deeper and deeper into the bug-infested wetland. I was pretty sure it was only my imagination that caused me to see movement within those shadows. At least I hoped it was my imagination and not a predator lurking under the cover of dense foliage.

"There," Cody said after what seemed like a lifetime. "I think this is the clearing where we're supposed to meet Baptiste." He looked at his watch. "He's supposed to be here at ten. It's nine-forty. We'll have to wait."

I considered our immediate surroundings. An owl hooted from atop a tall oak, while rodents and small mammals, hidden by low-growing foliage, scampered here and there. I was too afraid to stand in one place. Too afraid to go on. I'd faced down cold-blooded killers, yet they hadn't left me feeling quite so terrified as the nameless, faceless sounds in the night.

Cody took my hand and led me over to a fallen tree. He shone the flashlight over its surface before suggesting we sit down on it to wait. Sitting still in one place made me feel a bit like the goat that was tied to the tree in *Jurassic Park*, just waiting for an unseen predator to make him a tasty meal. Of course, in this particular situation, standing wasn't much better.

"What's that buzzing noise?" I whispered, afraid to allow even the sound of my own voice to penetrate the night.

"I'm not sure," Cody whispered back. "Perhaps insects of some sort. I've been in places with a similar hum, but this is quite unique."

"It almost sounds like a power tool. A saw or a grinder. I know it can't be, but that's what it sounds like."

"Maybe we can look it up online tomorrow," Cody suggested.

"It would be interesting to find out what's behind all those beady green eyes I keep seeing watching us. I wasn't expecting so much activity at night, but it seems as if the bayou is as full of life now as it is during the day. Maybe even more so."

I was quiet for a while, listening to my breath as it competed with the strange noises all around us. As it had been every night since we'd been in Louisiana, the heavy air was hot and moist. I wondered how people lived here. I supposed you had to get used to it, the way I was used to the cool nights and frequent rain of Madrona Island.

"And the bugs are the worst," I said as I slapped my neck as one of the voracious little vampires who lived in the moist undergrowth of the thick trees bit me. Normally, I wasn't bothered all that much by mosquitoes, but apparently, swamp mosquitoes found my Irish skin sweet and tasty. Cody had been slapping at himself for most of the journey, so I had the feeling we were both going to be covered in welts by the time the night was over. "How much longer?"

"About ten minutes," he answered.

I snuggled in closer to him, even though his body heat was as stifling as my own. Still, there was comfort to be found in his large frame. "I wonder how the cat knows," I said.

"Knows what?" Cody responded.

"Knows when it's ten o'clock. It's not like cats wear watches and tell time."

Cody turned and looked at me. "After everything you've seen the magical cats on the island do, you're wondering about that now?"

I let out a breath. "No. I guess not. I'm just really nervous sitting here. It helps to keep the conversation going."

Cody leaned over and kissed me on my forehead, even though it was covered in sweat. A true testament, I decided, to how much the man really loved me.

"I looked Abigail Beaumont up before we came out," Cody said, I was sure in an effort to keep my mind occupied.

"And?" I asked.

"The woman was brilliant and very beautiful, and she could be your twin. Even more so than the woman in the photograph in the gallery. It seems she had a big heart and a slightly reckless streak. She also was stubborn and strong-willed. I'm not saying I believe in reincarnation, but if I did, I wouldn't doubt for a moment that you shared a life force with that very remarkable woman."

I took a moment to consider that. The whole concept of reincarnation seemed pretty out there to me, but over the past couple of years I'd come to believe in some other pretty *out there* things. "She never married?"

"No, she didn't. She studied history and literature in college. After she graduated she became a teacher at a high school on the Gulf. Abigail loved the sea and wrote a series of essays about its beauty and danger using the pen name Andy Bradford. When she was twenty-five she published her first novel. She wrote four more during the course of her short life."

"How did she die?"

"When she was thirty-four she drowned off the coast of South Carolina while trying to save a young boy who'd been caught in a riptide."

I felt a catch in my throat. "Did the boy live?"

"Actually, he did. Abigail, or Abby, as she preferred to be called, was able to pull the boy onto a raft before she was caught up in the tide. A spectator on the beach was able to save the boy, but he couldn't get to Abby in time."

I suddenly felt like I was the one who couldn't breathe. I put a hand to my throat and inhaled deeply, filling my lungs with warm air.

"There he is." Cody stood and pointed into the distance. "The cat. The cat is Baptiste."

I willed my heart to slow as I waited for the cat to approach. I greeted him with a mixture of dread and relief. I wasn't sure I wanted to go where he was going to take us, but I did know I was ready for this night to be over. I glanced at Cody, who indicated I should go forward ahead of him, and we both set off after Baptiste.

After a few moments he left the trail we'd been following to wander even deeper into the dense wetland.

As the canopy of trees grew thicker, the light from the moon disappeared completely. The lack of even a small amount of natural light added to the eerie feel of the walk, but at least the cat seemed confident in his journey, which in an odd way gave me confidence as well. Over the past several years I had worked with more than a dozen cats on Madrona Island. Each had been sent by Tansy to help me solve whatever murder or mystery that had occurred at the moment. Most of the cats had disappeared from my life as abruptly as they had come into it, but each one had captured a piece of my heart and my soul.

"Do you think it's much farther?" I asked Cody as we trudged through the bayou. I wiped my wet brow with my wet arm, which really didn't seem to help. I felt like someone was slowly baking me to death.

"I don't know. The map Eden gave us ends at the point where we were to meet Baptiste. There's no way to know how much farther we'll need to travel now."

"What was that?" I jumped as a short scream penetrated the night.

Cody took my hand. "You don't want to know."

"But?"

"Don't think about it. Just keep walking."

I nodded. I supposed I could wager a guess as to which small creature had let out the forlorn scream, and I guess I didn't need Cody to spell out the circle of life for me. I knew how it worked, but Cody hadn't been wrong when he'd counseled me not to think about it.

"There." He pointed at a small cabin that literally was in the middle of nowhere.

"It looks dark."

"There was a flash in the window. I think it might have been a candle."

Cody and I followed the cat to the front door of the small building. I hoped he was going to stick around to lead us back to the car because I didn't think there was any way we could find our way back on our own. Of course, Cody had been trained as a Navy SEAL. He could probably retrace our steps himself if he had to.

"Should we knock?" I asked as the door slowly opened. I didn't see anyone standing on the other side of the door, so I pushed it open wider and took a tentative step inside. "Hello," I called out as the cat disappeared up some stairs.

"I've been expecting you." A tall woman with dark skin and white hair appeared from beyond the shadows.

"Jasmina?"

She nodded.

"We're here for the stone," I informed her.

"Come." Jasmina turned and walked toward the back of the structure. When she arrived at the back wall, a door appeared. She walked through it, indicating that I should follow her.

Okay, this was odd. The doorway didn't seem to lead anywhere. It was just an empty space filled with an eerie gray light. I didn't notice any of the scents or sounds of the bayou inside, and I wasn't able to make out any shape or forms beyond the light. After we'd taken several steps into this very strange void, Jasmina stopped. She held out her hands and said a chant of some sort, again in a language I didn't understand or recognize but suspected might be Haitian Creole. A blue stone that seemed more of a crystal appeared in Jasmina's hand. She turned and held it out toward me. I accepted the smooth, cool stone, which appeared to shimmer even in the dim light.

"This is the stone I'm to take to Tansy?"

Jasmina nodded. "The stone will restore the magic that has been lost. Tansy will know what to do with it."

I was about to thank her, but the next thing I knew I was standing on a path in the middle of the bayou. Cody was at my side, though there was no sign of Baptiste. "What in the heck happened? How did we get out here?"

"I've been waiting out here the whole time," Cody said.

I frowned. "What do you mean? Didn't you go with me into the cabin?"

Cody shook his head. "It disappeared the moment you stepped inside."

I frowned. "I'm sorry. I didn't realize you weren't right behind me."

"I tried to figure out how to follow you, but both you and the cabin were just... gone, so I waited for you."

"Well, that must have freaked you out a bit."

Cody smiled. "Before getting to know you better, I would have been terrified, but since coming back from the Navy I've seen so many amazing things happen on the island, having a cabin disappear with my fiancée inside it seemed like just another walk in the park. Was Jasmina inside the cabin? Do you have the stone? Are we all right to go back to the car?"

I nodded, feeling the weight of the stone in my hand, then showed it to him. "Can you find the car without Baptiste's help?"

Cody nodded. "I can."

"Okay, let's go."

Cody began to walk and I fell into step behind him. I focused on his broad shoulders and strong back and tried not to think about things that hummed and buzzed and went screech in the night. I thought of home and the life that awaited me on my return. My mom and four siblings, the new nephew we were about to welcome into the world. The bookstore I owned with my best friend, Tara, and the cats my aunt and I had been rescuing and housing in the Harthaven Cat Sanctuary for several years. This time in New Orleans had certainly been an adventure, but I couldn't wait to get home to the people and places I loved.

Madrona Island

I've spent my entire life on Madrona Island, the one farthest to the north and the west of all the islands in the San Juan chain. Born to an Irish Catholic family, I grew up in the blue-collar town of Harthaven, which was developed when twelve fishermen had settled in a colony there generations ago. I loved Madrona Island with all my heart and couldn't imagine living anywhere else. But the past few years had seen more change than the hundred before that, and at times I found myself pulled between the opposing forces of change and tradition. My great-great-grandfather was one of the founding fathers of Madrona. He'd worked hard, established a fishing business, and raised seven children. One by one, most of the descendants of those twelve founding families had left the island or died off, and now very few of us remained.

When the ferry began to stop on the island every day, its culture began to change dramatically. The town of Pelican Bay was established and the commercial fishing businesses that had created Madrona all but died, leading to the closing of the cannery and the loss of many jobs. That old economy gave way to a new one based on tourism, which continues to be a hot topic. I can understand both sides of the conflict. Like many members of the founding families, I have no desire to see condominiums rising up along the shore, destroying the natural beauty and solitude of the island. On the other hand, without the inflow of cash that tourists bring, most families, old and new, couldn't afford to stay on the island. Many have already been faced with the worst and have moved altogether.

As an adult, I've come to live in a world made up of boxes. There's the Sunday box, which I also think of as my Harthaven box. It includes the village of Harthaven, my mother, the church, and the Sunday dinner every Hart on the island is expected to attend each week. While I'd had a wonderful childhood filled with love and fond memories, there's a part of me that longs for something more than can be experienced in this blue-collar environment, where hard work, family, church, and tradition are the cornerstones of everyday life and are thought of being more than enough.

During the other six days of the week I live in the Pelican Bay box. Pelican Bay is a modern town that was built on the idea of personal enrichment, spiritual freedom, and economic prosperity, and its residents are an eclectic lot. That's where I co-own Coffee Cat Books with Tara O'Brian and share my life with wonderfully free-spirited souls, including a hippie couple, Banjo and Summer, who are most definitely stuck in the sixties, other neighbors from all walks of life, and my witchy friends, Bella and Tansy.

In the center of this magical place I call home is an area known as the hollow. It's a mystical place, where the magic Madrona Island is purported to possess seems to live. The hollow is uninhabited except for the feral cats who live in the dark spaces between the rocks. While most of the island's residents stop short of referring to the hollow as haunted, it's widely accepted that not everything that happens there can be explained.

The cats that inhabit the island are the main reason Cody and I had risked life and limb to obtain the magical rock Jasmina had assured me would restore the magic, which had somehow been lost. Our journey really had begun when Tansy had noticed cats were leaving the hollow for no apparent reason. We'd done some research and discovered the water in the hollow had been tainted. We'd thought if we could fix whatever was wrong with the water the cats would return and the magic would be restored, but that hadn't happened yet.

"Are you sure you don't want me to go on my own?" I asked Tansy as the trail narrowed and steepened. I had no idea how a woman who was all but bedridden by the time Cody and I returned from New Orleans with the blue crystal-like stone was able to come as far into the hollow as she already had.

Tansy paused and took a deep breath. "I'm fine. We must continue together. We'll need all the magic we both possess to place the stone in its rightful place."

I worried that Tansy seemed to be drawing on the last of her magic to put one foot in front of the other but continued. The trail was steep and covered in shale, making for a difficult and dangerous passage. I was in pretty good shape, so I was well equipped for a laborious hike, but I could sense a storm coming and was afraid it would arrive before Tansy and I could make our way back down the trail and out of the hollow. Still, I'd learned to trust her, so I kept on despite the risk. The trail narrowed as it wound steeply up the mountain. Even my legs burned as I struggled to keep my footing on the unstable ground.

As I walked, I looked for a sign that any of the islands cats were here now. No one knew for certain how the cats came to be here in the first place, but local legend had it that a man named Ivan Valtranova, a merchant from Russia, had found Madrona when he was blown off course during a storm. He took refuge in the hollow with the twelve cats with whom he'd traveled. If folklore is to be believed, he fell in love with the beauty and isolation of the island and decided to stay after the storm passed. Most assume the cats Valtranova brought with him were the base from which today's cat population had been bred.

According to the story, Valtranova lived alone on the island for a number of years, until the founding families arrived and built the fishing village that became Harthaven. It's said one of the settlers killed the Russian in a land dispute. Although the account of his demise had most likely been sensationalized, it did seem that after a hard-fought battle to regain his isolation, he was beheaded and his headless body was left in the hollow. The legend claimed the head was never found and is, in fact, buried somewhere in the hollow. There are those who believe the Russian's spirit is trapped there, and that he still wanders it, looking for his head and exacting his revenge on anyone who comes by night to disturb his solitude.

Personally, I'd always hoped the legend wasn't true. I didn't want to believe that one or more of the founding fathers had killed someone in cold blood to steal his land. And, although I visited the hollow regularly, I'd never been bothered by the Russian's or any other spirit. Of course, I made it a practice to be gone before sundown. But most legends are based at least in part on fact, and anyone who's lived on the island for any length of time will tell you there have been a number of strange and unexplained deaths on the island over the years.

"I can't help but think of the last time we came here together," I said as we continued to walk. "The cats had just begun to leave then. At the time I didn't think the solution to our problem would so difficult, but this has been a long and difficult journey that's been going on for months. Do you think this stone is really the answer?"

"I think it must be. Jasmina wouldn't offer a solution she wasn't certain would work."

I really hoped Tansy's faith hadn't been misplaced. I was worried about her, so I took my time, glancing behind me as I climbed the steep trail to make sure she was all right. I'd traveled this path many times before and knew the journey would become even more difficult before we reached the top of the bluff that overlooked the ground below. I'm not a witch and I don't claim to understand magic the way Tansy does, but it seemed to me that if two people with a connection to the magic were required to do whatever was needed today, it would have made more sense for Bella to come with me, with Tansy waiting for us back home in Pelican Bay. I'd gone so far as to suggest such a trade, but Tansy had insisted it was her journey to make.

After we reached the top of the bluff I stopped to look out over the view. The sun glistened off the still water of the ocean as seabirds glided above the surface, looking for their dinner. Despite the dark clouds on the horizon, I had the feeling of being able to see clear out to the edge of the world from the highest place on the island.

"The path down into the hollow will be brutal. Are you sure you don't just want to wait for me here?" I asked the increasingly pale and frail-looking witch.

"I'm sure. The journey is ours to make."

I took a deep breath and turned back toward the narrow path. "Okay. But let me know if you need to stop."

"I'll be fine, Caitlin Hart. Don't waste any energy worrying about me."

Easier said than done, I thought to myself as I slowly walked down the trail so as not to tax Tansy. "Here's the fork," I said after we'd been walking a while. "The same one we found the last time we were here. Then we went to the left, but both paths were narrow and both went inland. Should we go to the left once again or go to the right this time?"

"As before, I must instruct you to close your eyes and focus on the paths ahead of you," Tansy said.

Once again I did as she told me. Once again I asked myself which trail felt right, and once again I chose the path to the left. I just hoped I'd made the correct choice.

"We'll go to the left," I said with more confidence than I felt, and I turned and headed down that trail. I could feel Tansy walking behind me, but I could also sense her distress. I hoped our journey would come to an end soon.

Jasmina's instruction, which she had told me to relay to Tansy was to bring the stone into the hollow and find the cavern at the very center of the island. Once I'd found it, we were both to go inside. She'd warned me that the floor would drop sharply toward the bottom of the deep cavern, but we were to continue despite the effort required to complete the journey. When we reached the bottom we'd find an altar that, Jasmina said, had existed for centuries. It was on this altar that we must leave the stone after saying a few words, which Tansy knew. Jasmina had assured me that once the gift had been accepted, the cats would begin to return to their ancestral home.

"When Cody and I were in New Orleans we were sent on this crazy scavenger hunt that had us running all over the city for hours to find a map that, in my opinion, could have been presented to us in a much easier fashion. Do you have any idea why Jasmina or whoever drew it made things so hard?"

"It was a test," Tansy answered as we continued our descent toward the bottom of the hollow.

"A test?"

"I wasn't apprised of the details, but I do know it was important to Jasmina only to turn the stone over to someone who was worthy of it. The stone is a very powerful object and can be used for good or evil, depending on the intention of the person who possesses it. I think Jasmina just wanted to be sure you had what it took to be temporary guardian of it until it could be returned to its rightful place."

I chewed on that for a minute as we continued to walk. I supposed I understood the need for a test of some sort, but the one that had been provided for us had seemed pretty random and purposeless. "I don't understand how running around town following clues proved anything."

"Was it an enjoyable journey?" Tansy asked.

"Not at all. The weather was hot and humid, and I felt like I was swaddled in a wool blanket that was slowly suffocating me in itchy dampness. I can't remember the last time I was so uncomfortable physically."

"Yet you didn't quit despite your discomfort."

I bit my bottom lip as I navigated a particularly steep part of the trail. "No, I didn't quit. Trust me, I wanted to, but of course I wouldn't. It was too important."

"Your commitment to the journey despite personal sacrifice shows your willingness to put the needs of others before your own. That's an important trait for someone entrusted with magic."

I frowned. "I guess. It still seemed like a lot of hoopla to get a map."

"Were the clues easy to follow?" Tansy asked.

I shrugged. "Yes and no. It took some good, old-fashioned detective work to find a few of the locations we were sent to, but mostly the path wasn't too hard to follow. By the way, what was going on at Drusilla's magic shop? She wasn't really dead, was she?"

"Drusilla is fine."

I let out a breath of relief. "Good. I was worried when I saw all that blood. I was extra-freaked out when I saw the voodoo doll. She looked exactly like me. What was up with that?"

"I suppose it was just part of the test. There are many people who would have become overcome with fear at finding a voodoo doll that looked like them left in a puddle of blood. Most would have given up their quest right then and there."

I supposed Tansy had a point. I would probably have run and never looked back a few years ago, before I'd taken on the role of being a partner of the cats. I'd seen a lot of blood and a lot of death in those few years. I guess I wasn't as easily frightened as I once had been.

"Did you learn anything about yourself from your experience?" Tansy asked.

I thought of Abigail Beaumont. "Do you believe in reincarnation?"

Tansy paused to catch her breath. "Do you?"

I shook my head. "No. Not really. But this one thing did happen while we were in New Orleans. Cody and I met a woman in an art gallery. She offered to give us a tour, and since I was greedily enjoying her air-conditioning, I agreed. During the course of the tour she showed us a painting of an old plantation house. I swear to you, I recognized it. It wasn't like it looked similar to something I'd seen in the past; I was certain I'd seen that exact house. I've never been to Louisiana before, so having seen the house in person was pretty much impossible, yet I had a distinct memory of having been there."

Tansy didn't respond, so I continued telling her. "A short time later the gallery owner showed us a photo of the couple who'd lived in the house. I immediately knew the man's name was Pierre. It was really odd. She told us the couple had had a daughter, Abigail. The wife died shortly after Abigail was born and Pierre sent her to live with her maternal grandmother. As it turned out, she went on to lead a short but productive life. She died when she was thirty-four while trying to save the life of a young boy who was drowning."

"And you felt a connection to this woman?" Tansy asked.

"I did. The next day Cody showed me a photo of Abigail and she looked exactly like me. She could have been my twin. My logical mind acknowledges that we're both of Irish descent, so it isn't impossible that we could have similar features, but the other part of me, the part that's walking around in a magical place with a magical rock in my backpack, is telling me there's something more going on. I really feel like I was destined to find out about Abigail, but I don't have any idea why."

"Don't fret, Caitlin Hart. Your truth will come to you in time."

"I guess," I mumbled as I mulled over all the odd things that had happened to me in the past week. Life really was a wild ride when you allowed yourself to take the path less traveled. In my wildest dreams I never imagined that my trip to New Orleans and the Bayou would have turned out the way it had.

"And then there was the cat," I said, remembering Baptiste.

"You mean that cat?" Tansy stopped walking and pointed at the animal sitting on the trail ahead of us.

"Yes, that exact cat," I said and took a few steps forward. "How on earth did he get from Louisiana to here?"

Tansy didn't answer. I really hadn't expected her to. She was always closemouthed about how things with these magical cats actually worked and I didn't see why this should be an exception. "Never mind," I said. "I assume he wants us to follow him."

"That would seem to be the reason for his presence," Tansy agreed.

I paused to make sure Tansy was all right, then continued on as the cat went down the trail. "Have you ever been to the bayou?" I asked her after the trail leveled off a bit.

"I have not had the privilege."

"It's an odd sort of place," I began. "On one hand, it's beautiful and mysterious. Teeming with life, even in the middle of the night. I found sights, scents, and sounds there that seemed vaguely familiar, but in the end I couldn't identify them. In a way, the bayou felt as if it was alive. Not just the insects and animals that lived within it, but the whole area seemed to radiate its own energy. An odd sort of energy that both enticed and terrified me. I found I was enchanted and almost mesmerized by the sheer majesty of the place, yet it was also cruel and unyielding. It appeared to me that death comes as easily as life in the bayou. I've never experienced any place quite like it."

When Tansy didn't respond I stopped and turned around. She was standing completely still, her face as white as a sheet.

"Are you okay?" I asked.

"I rather think not."

"Should we stop?" I felt my pulse racing as I tried to figure out how best to help my friend.

"We must continue. I can feel the hollow screaming in pain. We must right what has been wronged."

"Maybe I should go on alone," I suggested worriedly.

"No. I must pass a test of my own. It won't be long now."

I really, really hated what was going on, but I nodded and kept walking, following Baptiste. Luckily, we didn't have far to travel before we reached the entrance to a cave. I knew the hike down would be steep, and I anticipated it might be narrow, so I insisted Tansy walk in front of me, so I could keep an eye on her.

As we slowly descended into the dark, cold interior of the cave, I was glad the cat had appeared and taken charge of the direction of the journey. I wasn't certain I would have entered the cave with Tansy in such bad shape if he hadn't been there to lead the way. Over the past few years I'd followed a number of magical cats into a variety of dangerous situations, but they'd never led me anywhere I couldn't ultimately handle.

"The path is getting steeper," Tansy warned me. "I think we're nearing the end to our journey."

As the path leveled off, the cave widened. At the bottom of the dark, narrow trail was what looked like a large chamber. In it was an altar built of rock. I turned around where I stood, looking at various scenes that had been painted on the dirt walls, depicting a time so long ago I found myself astonished at the fact that people had lived on the island that long ago. I wondered what had happened to those very first settlers. I knew that by the time the founding fathers arrived on Madrona Island it was all but deserted, except for the Russian.

"Do you have the stone?" Tansy asked.

I set my backpack on the ground and opened the top. I took out the stone and offered it to Tansy. She took the stone, said a few words I couldn't understand, then set it on the altar. As the blue stone I'd brought with me from the bayou settled on the stone of the altar, she took my hand. When we both touched the altar the cavern filled with light. I gasped.

"You feel it," Tansy said as energy seemed to radiate from her body.

"I do. It's amazing. I've never felt anything so powerful. So alive." I wasn't certain I was glowing the way Tansy was, but it certainly felt like it.

"You have the magic, just as I do. You always have. It's time, Caitlin Hart, for you to embrace your destiny."

Up Next from Kathi Daley Books

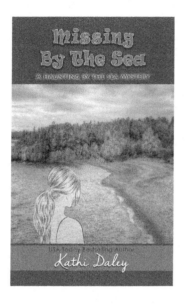

Preview of Missing By The Sea

Sunday, October 21

Life, I decided, was perfect. A sunny day, good friends, crisp weather, and an autumn forest brilliant with red, yellow, and even a hint of orange. Yes, I realized, as I walked across a rickety wooden bridge that spanned the river fed by the nearby falls beside my best friends, Mackenzie Reynolds and Trevor Johnson, life, in that moment, was exactly as I had always known it should be. Not that my life in New York City, where I'd lived until four months ago, hadn't been wonderful. It was just that after years of feeling torn between two worlds, I finally felt settled. Returning to Cutter's Cove, Oregon, the quaint seaside town where I'd lived for two years as a teenager while in witness protection, hadn't been part of my original plan, but when the death of a friend brought me back, I knew I'd never be able to leave.

"Oh look," Mac whispered as we neared the end of the swaying bridge.

I looked where she was pointing, at a doe and her fawn. They looked up and seemed to have sensed our presence yet hadn't run away. "They're beautiful," I replied in a soft voice, so as not to scare them. "I wish I had my camera." The red from the vine maples entwined with the yellow from the aspens against the evergreen of the forest presented the perfect backdrop for the deer perfectly framed in front of the lazy autumn waterfall.

"Maybe you can get a shot with your phone," Trevor suggested.

I decided to do what I could with that, but I knew the shot I really wanted to capture could only be realized with the lens and filters I'd decided I didn't want to carry on the short but steep hike up to the waterfall. I'd always enjoyed photography, but after moving back to Cutter's Cove, I'd decided to turn my hobby into a career by combining my work in graphic arts with the photographs I spent a good part of each week capturing.

"If the shot works out, I'd love to blow it up and hang it on the wall in my office," Mac said. Mac had moved into the oceanfront mansion my mother had gifted to me when I decided to make the move to the West Coast permanent. She had previously worked for a tech firm in California but had decided to take a risk and start her own company. Currently, she ran that company from her office on the third floor of my house.

I snapped the shot and then looked around. "Did anyone see where Sunny went?"

Sunny was one of the two dogs who lived with Mac and me, the other my German shepherd, Tucker. I hadn't wanted the dogs to scare the deer, so I'd made sure they stayed behind us. Tucker continued to wait in the exact spot where I'd told him to, but the much younger and not always obedient golden retriever I'd found on the side of the road and adopted appeared to have wandered off. I hated to scare the deer, which I knew would happen if I called for Sunny, but I didn't want to lose her in unfamiliar woods either.

"Sunny," I called after angling myself away from the deer.

My summons was met with barking.

"Sounds likes she doubled back and took the river path toward the falls," Trevor said.

I looked back to where the deer had been drinking to find them gone. "I'll get her." I turned around and headed back along the wooden bridge in the direction in which we'd just come. "Sunny," I called again. I was surprised she hadn't come when I'd called her the first time. She tended to become distracted at times, but it wasn't like her to completely ignore a command.

Once I arrived at the point where one could choose to take the wooden bridge or the narrow river trail, I headed along the river. I could hear Sunny moving around in the distance. I couldn't imagine what she'd found that had distracted her to the degree she'd apparently ignored me. "What do you have there?" I asked when I noticed she had something in her mouth. She dropped her prize at my feet. I felt my stomach lurch when I saw what she'd been carrying was a shoe. A bloody shoe.

I picked up the bright green tennis shoe and looked around. I didn't see anyone, but the blood on the shoe seemed fresh. "Hey, guys," I called to Mac and Trevor. "I think you'd better come over here."

"Did you find Sunny?" Mac called from across the river.

"I did. But I found something else as well. Something I think you both should see."

"On our way," Mac called.

I returned my attention to the forest surrounding me. It was then I spotted a movement behind the trees. I told Sunny to stay before walking slowly to where it seemed the movement had come from. "Is someone there?" I called out. I waited, but there was no reply. Remembering the bloody shoe, I continued with caution. "Are you in trouble? Do you need help?"

Again, I waited. After a moment I saw an object, or I suppose I should say a person, appear. "I won't hurt you," I said to the apparition.

"You can see me?" asked the ghost, who appeared to be a woman in her late teens or early twenties when alive.

"I can. My name is Amanda. Amanda Parker. What's your name?"

The image before me began to flutter and fade.

"I won't hurt you. I think I can help." I held up the shoe. "Does this belong to you?"

The vision became clearer. "I'm not sure."

I had the distinct feeling the ghost I was speaking to had died recently. Very recently.

"Everything feels so strange," the ghost said.

Mac and Trevor had walked up behind me. I motioned for them to stay back. "I suppose that's understandable."

"Am I dead?"

My heart filled with sympathy. "Yes. It appears you are."

The woman looked at her arm, which was defined but translucent. "I see. Do you know what happened to me?"

"No, I don't. But I can help you find out."

"How?"

"First, why don't you tell me your name and we can figure it out from there?"

The woman frowned. "I'm not sure." She looked around with an expression that reminded me of a frightened deer's. "I can't remember."

"Okay," I said in a soft voice. "That's okay. It isn't uncommon for spirits to become disoriented when they're first separated from their bodies. Maybe we should start by finding your body. Do you remember where you left it?"

The woman faded away. I decided to wait. My sense was that she wanted to find her answers and just needed a moment to gather her thoughts. Eventually, the image returned. Once again, I asked her to lead me to the place where she'd left her body.

"I can't remember," she said. "Everything is so fuzzy. I can't remember who I am or how I got here."

"Okay," I assured her. "Don't fade away." I gestured behind me. "These are my friends. Mac and

Trevor. They'll help me look for your body. I have a feeling it's close by. Is that all right with you?"

She looked as if she might flee but then nodded. I turned and looked at Mac and Trevor. "I've made contact with a spirit. I would estimate she was in her late teens or early twenties when she passed, and I'm fairly certain that happened recently. She can't remember her name or where her body is, so we're going to help her look for it." I held up the bloody shoe. "I believe this belonged to her. Sunny had it in her mouth when I found her, so I expect the body is close by."

"What do you want us to do?" Trevor asked.

"I want the two of you to take Tucker and continue upstream. I'm going to take Sunny and head off into the woods in the direction I first saw the image appear. Yell if you find anything and I'll do the same. If you don't find anything within a half mile, turn around and come back here."

I called to Sunny and set off into the woods. The ghost seemed content to float along with me. She looked so young. It broke my heart that she most likely had come to a violent end. "Can you remember anything at all yet?" I asked as we walked.

She fluttered in and out but stayed with me. I could sense her confusion. "No." The ghost paused and looked around. "Everything is out of focus."

"Maybe we should start by your telling me anything you do remember."

She took another moment before she began to speak slowly. "I remember seeing the dog with the shoe. I wondered if it was my shoe, and where she'd gotten it. I was trying to remember where I was and how I got here when you called for the dog. I waited for you in the hope you'd be able to help me."

I glanced at Sunny, who was patiently waiting for us to continue our walk. "I don't know what happened to you yet, but I'll help you find out."

"It doesn't seem right that I'm here."

"Why is that?" I asked as I started walking once again, picking my way through the forest as I made my way deeper into the brush.

"I don't know exactly. It just feels wrong. I don't think I've been here before. Nothing is familiar."

"You might just be feeling displaced because of the recent trauma." I looked down at Sunny. She hadn't been trained in search and rescue, but we did play hide and seek. I held the bloody tennis shoe up to her nose. "Find the other one, Sunny. Find the shoe."

Sunny began wagging her whole body. She must think we were going to play a game. She took off running in the opposite direction from which I'd been walking. I didn't have a better idea, so I followed. It didn't take long for her to find a spot in the woods where the ground had recently been disturbed. Sunny started to dig, but I called her away and told her to stay.

"I found something," I called as loudly as I could, hoping Mac and Trevor would hear me. A few breaths later, I heard them call back that they were on their way.

"Is that it?" the woman asked. "Is that where I'm buried?"

"I think so," I answered. "We won't know for sure until we dig it up. I'm not sure you should be here for this."

"I don't want to be alone."

I found myself wishing Alyson were here, and suddenly she was. I hadn't seen her in over two months and had thought she was gone for good. I was happy to see she wasn't. Alyson was my alter ego who I'd first discovered on returning to Cutter's Cove this summer. I'd learned she was the part of me I'd left behind when I'd returned to New York ten years ago. Initially, she'd existed as an apparition I could see and talk to, but when I decided to stay in Cutter's Cove, the two of us had become integrated, and most of the time she existed on the inside. She had a way of showing up when I needed her most, however.

"I'll wait with you," Alyson said to the ghost, taking her hand.

"Are you dead too?" the ghost asked.

"No. It's a long story. Come with me and I'll tell you about it."

"Don't go far," I cautioned as Alyson and the ghost disappeared from sight.

I walked toward what I was sure was the shallow grave of a murder victim. There was a trail of blood leading to it. If I had to guess, I'd say the girl had been injured while being pursued by her killer. My chest clenched as my heart broke for someone whose life had been stolen from her much too soon.

"Oh no," Mac said when she arrived and noticed the mound of dirt.

"It looks like you found your ghost's body," Trevor said. He looked around. "Is she still here?"

"Alyson took her somewhere. I'm sure they're nearby. Should we dig ourselves or call Woody?"

"I'd call Woody and wait for him," Mac said.

I held up my phone. "No bars."

"I have a satellite phone," Mac said and took it out. "I'll walk back to that meadow we passed; I should have reception there. I'll have Woody take the waterfall trail and meet us at the foot of the bridge. We can wait for him there and lead him to this spot."

"Yeah, okay. That's a good idea."

"There sure is a lot of blood," Trevor said as we headed to the meadow.

"Yeah." I sighed. "I have a feeling she met with a very violent end."

"Can she remember anything?" Mac asked as we made our way back through the forest.

"She doesn't remember anything that happened before she found herself in the woods watching Sunny with her bloody shoe," I answered. "If her death was as traumatic as it appears, she might be repressing it."

"From the damage to the foliage back there, she must have been chased or pursued," Trevor said.

"I had the same thought," I agreed. "Woody should have some idea."

By the time he arrived with two officers and the body had been dug up, bagged, and taken away, the sun had set and it was close to dark. The area had been sectioned off with crime scene tape and two men in plain clothes had shown up to gather samples and look for physical evidence. The young woman had definitely died from a gunshot wound to the back, and based on the cuts and abrasions on her arms, legs, and feet, it looked as if she'd run through the forest beforehand.

"Any idea who she is?" Woody asked after he'd finished speaking to the men who'd recently arrived.

I shook my head. "She couldn't remember."

"She *couldn't remember*?"

"The woman who was killed. The reason I even knew to look for the body in the first place was because I stumbled across her ghost. Unfortunately, when I asked her who she was she couldn't remember. I think she has amnesia."

"Amnesia?" Woody looked doubtful but eventually shrugged. "Okay. The crime scene guys are going to take over now. I'm heading back to the office. I'll see if I can figure out who the victim is. I'll call you once I get an ID."

"Thanks. And thanks for responding so quickly."

"It's my job," he reminded me.

Of course it was his job to recover the bodies of murder victims, but it wasn't his job to suspend disbelief when fed a story about amnesiac ghosts, but he did it anyway. When he left and the crime scene guys moved on to check out the perimeter, I called to Alyson. She reappeared, along with the woman whose body had just been found.

"What happened?" she asked.

"You were shot and buried here, but it appears you ran through the woods before that, I imagine to escape your killer. Do you have any idea at all where you were prior to being here?"

She shook her head, looking interested but not overly traumatized. I had a feeling she hadn't quite made the connection between her current state and the body that had just been taken away. "Do you know who I am?"

"Not yet, but we'll find out. It's important that you move on to the next life now that your spirit has departed. I think Alyson can help you do that."

She shook her head. "Not until I know. I don't remember who I was, but I have to assume there are people who cared about me. I need to be sure they get the answers they need. Once I'm certain they're okay, I can move on."

I glanced at Alyson, who shrugged. "Okay," I said. "I suggest you come home with us until we have your answers. Alyson can show you the way. Is that all right with you?"

She nodded. "Yes."

Alyson and the woman disappeared. I wasn't sure how either Alyson or the ghosts I had come into contact with moved through time and space; they seemed to be where they wanted or needed to be.

"Let's go," I said to Mac and Trevor. "Alyson is taking her to the house."

"I'm kind of surprised she showed up again," Trevor said. "Didn't you think she was gone for good?"

I shrugged. "I have no idea how it works. I haven't seen her for two months but today, when I needed her, she was willing and able to help."

"You can ask Chan about it," Mac said, referring to our friend, who owned a magic shop and seemed to be a lot better versed in all things supernatural than I.

"I will. It'd be nice to know I can count on her when I need her."

It was completely dark by the time we hiked out of the forest and returned to the house. I fed both dogs, then went in search of my cat, Shadow, who, interestingly enough, could see both Alyson and the ghosts who came into my life. His ability has helped me on more than one occasion.

Trevor offered to start dinner while I went upstairs to try to connect with Alyson and the ghost. If Woody didn't come up with a name pretty quickly, we'd need to assign her a temporary one. Continuing to call her *the ghost* would become awkward. Mac had gone up to her office to check her emails and to call Ty Matthews, the man she was romantically interested in, though she'd only admit to him being her business partner. I figured I had at least twenty minutes of quiet time.

"Alyson, are you here?" I called.

After a moment, she appeared.

"Is our ghost friend with you?"

"She is." Alyson looked to her side. "You can appear. It's safe here."

"Did you find out who I am?" she asked.

"Not yet. But we're working on it. In the meantime, are you okay with Alyson?"

She nodded.

"Is there a name we can use to refer to you? Something temporary name, until you learn your real name?"

"Anything is fine."

I glanced at her. "Is there a name that comes to you? One tickling the corner of your mind?"

"Sissy. I think I was called Sissy, although I don't think it was my name."

"Sissy is a good name. That's what we'll call you until you remember your real name. I don't expect to hear from the police for a while yet. I'm not sure how time and space work exactly where you are, but feel free to hang around here. I'll make sure you know it when I have news to share."

"Okay. And thank you. It will be nice to remember."

As Alyson and Sissy faded away, I headed downstairs to join Trevor in the kitchen. My mom had gone back to New York for a few months but had plans to return to Cutter's Cove for Christmas. Mac and I had settled into a routine of either picking up takeout or making something simple for dinner on most nights, but when Trevor wasn't working, he usually cooked for us. Sometimes we dined at his home on the beach, other times he did the honors in my kitchen, but wherever the food was made, you could bet it was going to be wonderful.

"Smells like garlic," I said to my tall, dark-haired friend as I poured myself a glass of wine and sat down at the kitchen counter.

Trevor shot me a half grin. "I'm making a seafood chowder with the shrimp, crab, and scallops I found in your freezer. It's quick and hearty, with potatoes and carrots and seafood simmered in a lemon garlic broth. Do you have any bread we can heat up? This is the sort of dish you'll want to eat with bread for dipping."

"I have several loaves of heat-and-serve bread in the freezer. Not as good as fresh, but pretty good in a pinch. Mac and I don't cook a lot, so I haven't been keeping fresh ingredients on hand. Maybe we can go into town tomorrow to pick up some fresh seafood and greens from the farmers market, and bread from the bakery."

"That sounds great," Trevor tasted the broth, then added several spices from my mother's rack. "Have you heard from Woody? We talked about heading to Dooley's Farm tomorrow to pick up the pumpkins for

205

the decorations for the fund-raiser, but I wasn't sure how the arrival of the newest ghost in our lives might impact that."

"I haven't heard from him. If I don't by the time we finish eating dinner, I'll call him. Unless there's a missing persons report or some other readily available way to identify her, it might not be all that easy."

Trevor turned the heat down and covered the pot. "Someone must be missing her."

"I agree. Sissy seems to be very concerned with finding out who she is so she can make sure the people she might have left behind know what happened to her."

"She remembered her name?"

"No. Sissy is a temporary name. I figured if she didn't remember her real name soon, we'd be stuck calling her *the ghost* for who knows how long." I got up and crossed the room to click on the gas fire in the fireplace built into the back wall of the kitchen. When Mom and I bought the house, the fireplace had used logs, but when we remodeled we switched to gas. The only fireplace in the house that still used real wood was the one in the living room.

"I've been thinking it might be fun to convert that fireplace into a brick pizza oven. It wouldn't be all that difficult to do, and you've been looking for ways to make the space yours," Trevor suggested.

"I love the idea, but I don't know how to make pizza. If I do convert it, you'll have to come over and make use of it."

"Seems like I'm over here every night I'm not working anyway. The oven could still be used as an accent piece even when you weren't making pizza. We'd create a large arched opening here." Trevor outlined the area with his hand. "The flames inside the oven would be visible from the seating area and could be turned on whether you were cooking or not. In fact, I've seen brick pizza ovens with a larger opening lower in the brick for a regular fireplace, then a smaller opening for the pizza oven above that. I can draw you a design if you're interested."

"Yeah, do it. It sounds like a lovely idea. I've been thinking about building a wine cellar in the basement, or at least part of the basement. Between that and the pizza oven, the house will take on an old-world Italian feel. At least this part of the house anyway. I'm not sure why, but that appeals to me."

Trevor placed the bread on a cookie sheet and popped it in the oven. "I love the idea of a wine cellar. The space isn't being used right now, so you may as well add some charm and functionality to it. I can build you wine racks when you're ready. I have some repurposed wood that would work really well."

"Sounds awesome. It'd be fun to go wine tasting and select some bottles once we finish the space."

"There are a ton of really great wineries in the Willamette Valley. I went with a group a few years ago. We made a weekend of it and had the best time. Maybe the three of us could work out a tour. There are some really nice bed-and-breakfasts in the area."

"Sounds like fun."

"This will be ready in about fifteen minutes. I'll run up to let Mac know. The soup is on simmer, so it should be fine until I get back, but you might want to keep your eye on the bread."

I took a peek at the bread, which looked to have at least another fifteen minutes, then wandered onto the deck. It was a cold but clear night, with just a hint of a breeze. The sound of the waves crashing onto the rocks below was somewhat muted, indicating to me that the tide was most likely low. I'd stood out on this deck listening to the waves and looking at the stars overhead hundreds of times before. I was happiest and most at home on this deck, but tonight I felt a lingering sadness as I thought about Sissy and the life that had been taken from her much too soon. I couldn't imagine what had happened to her. Given the number of scrapes and abrasions on her body, it looked as if she'd run heedlessly through the forest for quite some time before being gunned down.

"It's dark." Alyson suddenly appeared next to me.

"Yes. I can see that."

"No, I don't mean the sky. It's Sissy. Her mind is dark."

I frowned. "You can see into her mind?"

"Not really." Alyson frowned. "Well, sort of. It's hard to explain."

"Can you see what happened to her?" I asked.

"I can't tell you what happened to her, but I can tell you that any memories she's had have been wiped clean. It's as if she never even existed before today."

Okay, that was strange. At least I thought it was strange. I was no expert on either amnesia or ghosts, but I guess I assumed her memories were there but inaccessible. "Maybe her memories will come back with time. I'm going to do everything I can to help her find her answers. It must be so strange not to remember anything from her life."

"I'm sure she finds it unsettling."

I smiled at Alyson. "I'm glad you're here. I've missed you."

"I'm always here with you, only on the inside. I'm looking forward to the fund-raiser. We'll need a new dress."

"The masquerade ball is going to be a big deal. If things go as planned, Caleb is hoping to raise enough money to expand the children's wing at the hospital."

Caleb Wellington, along with his fiancée, Chelsea Green, had set up a charitable foundation with part of the money he'd inherited from his grandfather, Barkley Cutter. Both Caleb and Chelsea had grown up in Cutter's Cove and had deep ties to the place. It was here, they'd decided, they'd share their wealth and raise a family. The idea for the masquerade ball was Chelsea's, but once Caleb had latched onto it, he'd made it his own by incorporating the props he'd developed over the years working on the annual Halloween Haunted Hayride. The ball was set to take place in the house philanthropist Booker Oswald had donated to the historical society. In addition to providing an elegant affair, Caleb planned to create an enchanted environment similar to that of a haunted mansion. I thought the event was going to be spectacular.

"I was thinking a simple but elegant long black dress with a black sequined mask," Alyson continued. "We might even want to consider a long black wig to give our costume the Morticia Addams feel. Not that people are necessarily dressing up, but I think a wig would be fun."

I chuckled. "Do you know how odd it is for me to be having a conversation with myself?"

Alyson smiled and shrugged. "Stranger things have happened to us."

"I guess that's true. I'm not sure about the wig, but a long black dress sounds great. We'll go shopping this week."

"Tomorrow?"

"No. Not tomorrow," I answered. "I'm hoping to work on Sissy's murder case, and we're supposed to help Chelsea decorate tomorrow. The ball isn't until Saturday, so we'll have plenty of time to run over to Portland and look for a dress." I glanced at the door. "I think Trev has dinner ready. Keep an eye on Sissy and let me know if she begins to remember."

"I will, but I don't think she will. At least not without help."

"Then we'll find a way to help her. Maybe Mac can run her image though her facial recognition program if Woody can give us a photo. It's a long shot, but it might turn something up. In the meantime, there's a bowl of seafood chowder and a glass of wine with my name on it."

I turned around to go back inside when a chill ran down my spine. I looked around but didn't see anything out of place. Still I had one of those distinct feelings you get when you're being watched. I could see the ocean in the distance and the wide-open feel of the meadow leading up to the edge of the bluff. Both appeared to be empty. It was dark, so I couldn't see anything beyond the tree line in the distance, but I doubted anyone was there. I might just be spooked after what had happened today. After all, a young woman was dead, and as far as I knew, her killer was still out there.

Recipes

Cabbage Soup—submitted by Nancy Farris
Mom's Mexican Cornbread—submitted by Darla Taylor
Corn and Chicken Stew—submitted by Taryn Lee
Pumpkin Cake—submitted by Pam Curran

Cabbage Soup

Submitted by Nancy Farris

Think deconstructed cabbage rolls in soup form! It will warm you up on a cool day.

1 lb. ground beef
1 med. onion, chopped
2 cloves garlic, minced
1 qt. beef broth
1 can Rotel tomatoes
1 can 28-oz. crushed tomatoes
1 bay leaf
Salt and pepper to taste
½ head med.-size cabbage, chopped
Cooked rice

Brown beef, add onion and garlic, and cook about 3–4 minutes. Add broth, all tomatoes, and bay leaf. Salt and pepper to taste. Bring to boil, lower heat to low, and cook for 30 minutes. Add chopped cabbage and cook another 30 minutes over low heat.

During the last 30 minutes, make your rice (do not use instant rice; it gets mushy) separately. When it's done, add it to the soup for the last 5 minutes. Add more salt and pepper if needed.

Serve with warm, crusty bread.

Mom's Mexican Cornbread

Submitted by Darla Taylor

Batter:
½ cup flour
1 cup cornmeal
1 can creamed corn
1 cup whole milk
½ cup shortening
1 tsp. baking powder
½ tsp. baking soda
¾ tbs. salt
2 eggs

Filling:
½ cup longhorn cheese, shredded
½ lb. ground beef, cooked
1 large white onion, chopped
3–4 jalapeños (or green and/or red peppers), chopped or sliced

Preheat oven to 350 degrees. Mix the batter. Set aside layer ingredients. Grease a large cast-iron skillet. Pour in half of the batter. Top batter with cheese, then the ground beef, followed by the onion and peppers. Top with remaining batter. Bake for 45–50 minutes.

Corn and Chicken Stew

Submitted by Taryn Lee

1 med. onion
3 cloves garlic
1 tbs. vegetable oil
1 cup carrot, finely chopped
2 cups fresh or frozen corn
2 cans chicken broth
12 oz. shredded, fully cooked, seasoned chicken
(rotisserie chicken from the store will do if you don't
have time to prepare your own)
Salt to taste
Pepper to taste
1 cup chopped ripe tomatoes (canned will do in a
pinch)
2 cups freshly grated Parmesan cheese
¼ cup fresh cilantro, chopped
Lime wedges (optional)

Chop onion and mince garlic.

Over med.-high heat, heat oil in large skillet and sauté
onion and carrot until onion is clear, about 5 minutes.

Add corn and garlic to skillet, then sauté 3–5 minutes
or until corn is golden and other vegetables are
browned.

Add chicken broth to skillet and bring vegetable mixture to a boil. Add shredded chicken, stirring until it is heated.

Season with salt and pepper to taste.

Serve stew in bowls and top with the tomatoes, Parmesan, and cilantro. If desired, place a lime wedge as a condiment to serve with stew.

Pumpkin Cake

Submitted by Pam Curran

4 eggs
2 cups sugar
1 cup cooking oil
2 cups flour
2 tbs. cinnamon
2 tsp. soda
½ tsp. salt
2 cups pumpkin (1 can)

Cream eggs and sugar; add oil. Mix dry ingredients together and add to creamed mixture. Add pumpkin at low speed of mixer. Bake in greased, floured Bundt pan at 350 degrees for 1 hour.

Frosting:
8 oz. cream cheese
1 stick butter, softened
½ box confectioner's sugar(sifted)
1 tsp. vanilla

Mix all together and spread on cooled cake.

Books by Kathi Daley

Come for the murder, stay for the romance

Zoe Donovan Cozy Mystery:

Halloween Hijinks
The Trouble With Turkeys
Christmas Crazy
Cupid's Curse
Big Bunny Bump-off
Beach Blanket Barbie
Maui Madness
Derby Divas
Haunted Hamlet
Turkeys, Tuxes, and Tabbies
Christmas Cozy
Alaskan Alliance
Matrimony Meltdown
Soul Surrender
Heavenly Honeymoon
Hopscotch Homicide
Ghostly Graveyard
Santa Sleuth
Shamrock Shenanigans
Kitten Kaboodle
Costume Catastrophe
Candy Cane Caper
Holiday Hangover
Easter Escapade
Camp Carter
Trick or Treason
Reindeer Roundup
Hippity Hoppity Homicide

Firework Fiasco
Henderson House
Holiday Hostage – *December 2018*

Zimmerman Academy The New Normal
Ashton Falls Cozy Cookbook

Tj Jensen Paradise Lake Mysteries by Henery Press:

Pumpkins in Paradise
Snowmen in Paradise
Bikinis in Paradise
Christmas in Paradise
Puppies in Paradise
Halloween in Paradise
Treasure in Paradise
Fireworks in Paradise
Beaches in Paradise

Whales and Tails Cozy Mystery:

Romeow and Juliet
The Mad Catter
Grimm's Furry Tail
Much Ado About Felines
Legend of Tabby Hollow
Cat of Christmas Past
A Tale of Two Tabbies
The Great Catsby
Count Catula
The Cat of Christmas Present
A Winter's Tail
The Taming of the Tabby
Frankencat

The Cat of Christmas Future
Farewell to Felines
A Whisker in Time
The Catsgiving Feast – *November 2018*

Writers' Retreat Mystery:
First Case
Second Look
Third Strike
Fourth Victim
Fifth Night
Sixth Cabin
Seventh Chapter

Rescue Alaska Paranormal Mystery:
Finding Justice
Finding Answers
Finding Courage
Finding Christmas – *December 2018*

A Tess and Tilly Mystery:
The Christmas Letter
The Valentine Mystery
The Mother's Day Mishap
The Halloween House
The Thanksgiving Trip – *October 2018*

Haunting by the Sea:
Homecoming by the Sea
Secrets by the Sea
Missing by the Sea – *October 2018*

The Inn at Holiday Bay:
Boxes in the Basement – *November 2018*

Sand and Sea Hawaiian Mystery:
Murder at Dolphin Bay
Murder at Sunrise Beach
Murder at the Witching Hour
Murder at Christmas
Murder at Turtle Cove
Murder at Water's Edge
Murder at Midnight

Seacliff High Mystery:
The Secret
The Curse
The Relic
The Conspiracy
The Grudge
The Shadow
The Haunting

Road to Christmas Romance:
Road to Christmas Past

USA Today best-selling author Kathi Daley lives in beautiful Lake Tahoe with her husband Ken. When she isn't writing, she likes spending time hiking the miles of desolate trails surrounding her home. She has authored more than seventy-five books in eight series, including Zoe Donovan Cozy Mysteries, Whales and Tails Island Mysteries, Sand and Sea Hawaiian Mysteries, Tj Jensen Paradise Lake Series, Writers' Retreat Southern Seashore Mysteries, Rescue Alaska Paranormal Mysteries, and Seacliff High Teen Mysteries. Find out more about her books at **www.kathidaley.com**

Stay up-to-date:
Newsletter, *The Daley Weekly*
http://eepurl.com/NRPDf
Webpage – **www.kathidaley.com**
Facebook at Kathi Daley Books –
www.facebook.com/kathidaleybooks
Kathi Daley Books Group Page –
https://www.facebook.com/groups/569578823146850/
E-mail – **kathidaley@kathidaley.com**
Twitter at Kathi Daley@kathidaley –
https://twitter.com/kathidaley
Amazon Author Page –
https://www.amazon.com/author/kathidaley
BookBub –
https://www.bookbub.com/authors/kathi-daley

Made in the USA
Middletown, DE
17 October 2018